VIGILANTES AND LOVERS

THE J.R. FINN SAILING MYSTERY SERIES

C.L.R. DOUGHERTY

VIGILANTES AND LOVERS

The J.R. Finn Sailing Mystery Series
Book 3

Intrigue and Romance in the Caribbean

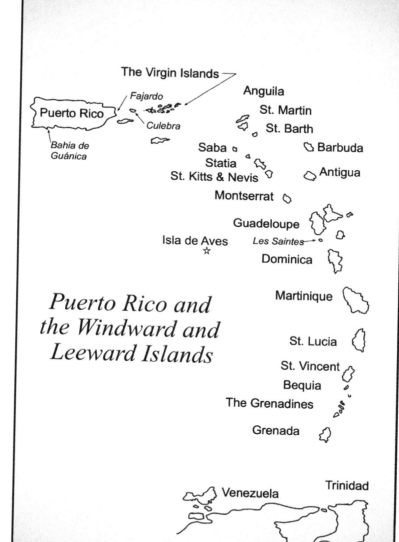

The Virgin Islands

Fajardo

Puerto Rico

Culebra

Bahia de
Guánica

Anguila

St. Martin

St. Barth

Saba

Statia

St. Kitts & Nevis

Montserrat

Barbuda

Antigua

Guadeloupe

Isla de Aves

Les Saintes

Dominica

*Puerto Rico and
the Windward and
Leeward Islands*

Martinique

St. Lucia

St. Vincent

Bequia

The Grenadines

Grenada

Venezuela

Trinidad

1

Before my flight left Miami, I decided to kill Nora. Five hours later, I was back in Tortola aboard *Island Girl*, my sailboat and my home, with Nora on my mind.

I put my thoughts of her aside long enough to clear out with Her Majesty's Customs for an overnight sail to St. Martin. In St. Martin I could buy things I couldn't find elsewhere, at least not in the islands. Things I would need, given my decision to kill Nora.

Clearance in hand, I was underway and out in open water. I would sail through the night and make my landfall in Simpson Bay in time for the first drawbridge into St. Martin's lagoon.

Sailing alone at night is one of my favorite times for thinking and planning. My thoughts returned to Nora.

Killing Nora wasn't a casual undertaking. She occupied a prominent place in my life — Nora, or Phyllis Greer, or whatever she was calling herself that day. After 20 years, I didn't even know her real name. So I settled on calling her Nora.

She showed her true nature when Mary came into my life. Nora was about my age; Mary wasn't much older than my daughter.

Midlife crisis? Not me. Just because an attractive young woman disrupted my comfortable, well-ordered life, I wasn't buying into that cliché. My situation was different.

When I first took up with Mary, I thought she was just a diversion. A diversion for me, and a red herring for my opponents. When I met her, I was leaving Puerto Rico on a classified mission. Setting sail to St. Vincent and the Grenadines, I had orders to kill a scumbag operating out of a bar in Kingstown, St. Vincent. But that's a whole different story.

Mary was standing on the dinghy dock in Puerto Real when I went ashore for a little last-minute grocery shopping before leaving Puerto Rico. She offered to buy me a drink, and before I knew what happened, she talked me into taking her along to the Grenadines. That was a four-day sail, just the two of us, alone and out of sight of land.

What happened between us on the voyage wasn't surprising. Being attacked before we left Puerto Real coupled with what happened when we got to the Grenadines — that was surprising. But as I said about my mission, that's yet another story.

Nora knew about Mary before Mary found out about Nora. But predictably, they both caught on before it was over. Nora's first reaction was amusement. She even encouraged my pursuit of Mary; Nora wanted to include Mary in *our* relationship. That wasn't what it sounds like.

By the time we reached the Grenadines, Mary and I were lovers. Nora and I were not — we never were. Until a few weeks ago, Nora was just a voice on the phone. I didn't even meet her face-to-face until *after* I took up with Mary.

Before I retired, Nora was my boss. She ran an obscure little government agency that was completely off the books. When Nora took over, I was one of the newer members of the agency; by the time I retired, Nora and I were the people with the longest tenure.

Attrition was a problem among assassins, but I was the best they had. I survived to retire, and they gave me contract work after that.

They found it useful to have a reliable killer living on a sailboat in the Caribbean. A lot of bad characters ended up passing through the islands, along with a bunch of boat bums who looked like me. I was invisible down here — just another middle-aged dropout scratching out a life on a battered old sailboat.

And that was how I met Mary. Aside from teasing me a little, she was okay when she found out about Nora. Neither of them seemed to feel threatened by the other, and I didn't see why they should.

Two open-minded women? How lucky could a man get? But things like that never last. Our odd, three-way relationship was unraveling.

The story of Nora and Mary and me wasn't over yet. Nora was trying to work her way back into my life, but I wasn't going to let that happen.

I learned some disturbing things about Nora in the last several days. After working for her for nearly 20 years, I found out she was a crook. Not only was Nora a crook, but she betrayed me in a way I couldn't forgive.

It might end my long relationship with the U.S. government, but I was going to kill her. Nora's death would be the best thing for everyone I cared about. I just needed to work out the details of her demise.

2

I WAS WELL CLEAR OF THE VIRGIN ISLANDS AND ON COURSE
for St. Martin. There wasn't much traffic to keep me awake.
That's one of the challenges of single-handed voyaging.
Having Mary aboard to stand watches spoiled me over the
last few weeks. Too bad she was busy in Florida for a
while yet.

I missed her, and not just because she was good crew.
Despite the difference in our ages, Mary and I thought alike.
We shared the same profession.

She didn't work for the government, though, and that
was a critical difference, at least in my mind. She was a
hired killer. Mary recently took out several high-level
mobsters.

Everybody has a boss — even high-level mobsters. The
mobsters' bosses weren't pleased with Mary. She became a
target in her own right, which was why she hitched a ride
with me to begin with. She was on the run when we left
Puerto Rico, although I didn't know it then.

And the people chasing her wanted more than revenge.

Two of the mobsters she killed were laundering money. Mary stole their files.

The files went beyond simple bookkeeping; they included long, detailed lists of corrupt politicians and government employees. The files were encrypted, so nobody except the guilty ones knew whose names were on the list.

Those guilty ones wanted Mary dead, but not until they recovered the files from her. And because I was keeping company with her, they came after me, too.

One of their minions, a corrupt FBI agent named Kelley, almost disrupted my last mission for Nora. I asked Nora to check him out.

The backlash from her research was swift. Nora told me she was fired as the result of her asking questions about Kelley.

After Nora supposedly lost her job over the questions about Kelley, she arranged to meet me in St. Thomas. She wanted to recruit me and Mary to work with her in a new venture to clean up the corruption we uncovered.

The St. Thomas meeting was a setup. The intent was to make me turn over Mary and the files. It backfired on Nora, and people died.

When they didn't get what they wanted from the St. Thomas meeting, the crooks kidnapped my daughter, Abby. That pissed me off and cemented my relationship with Mary.

She and I set out to avenge Abby, and we did. Our retribution was deadly. They wouldn't underestimate us again.

In the aftermath, Nora called me, which was a big surprise. Until her phone call, I thought she was killed as part of the setup.

She was feigning innocence when she called, but the call reminded me she could track me using a special satellite phone she gave me. I destroyed the phone.

For 20 years, Nora never misled me, but now there wasn't much doubt about her taking direction from the people trying to kill me and Mary. Nora was a rogue agent.

As a result of Mary's help freeing my daughter, I learned that Mary was connected with a shadowy, powerful man. In response to a call from her, he helped us rescue Abby.

So far, Mary wasn't willing to talk about him, not that I could blame her. We weren't sharing all our professional secrets yet. Maybe we never would.

For the moment, Mary and I were on the same side, but I couldn't help worrying about her relationship with that mysterious man. Phorcys, she called him. And he called her Medusa. She said those were passcodes, not pseudonyms.

I wondered, though. Phorcys and his sister Ceto were figures from Greek mythology. In some versions of their story, Medusa was their daughter. When I asked her if Phorcys was her father, Mary evaded the question.

I wouldn't read anything into that. Both of us were evasive from habit; it was a survival skill in our business. Still, she did have a tattoo of Medusa on her hip.

When we were last together, Mary let me listen in on her phone calls with Phorcys. Their exchanges were businesslike; there was no personal innuendo.

Phorcys was indebted to her; that was clear. She said it was because she handled some sensitive work for him. I probed a little, fishing for a personal connection, but she didn't take the bait.

As far as I could tell, she didn't let him know I was in on

the calls. That meant something important, either for me, or for him. I wasn't sure which, yet.

It wasn't that I didn't trust Mary; we were past that. I trusted her as much as I trusted anybody, which wasn't much.

That was part of what kept me alive. But I didn't think Mary meant me harm, at least not right now.

Nevertheless, I wanted to know more about Phorcys. He might be indebted to Mary, but he owed me nothing, and he knew at least something about me from Mary. That could make him dangerous to me.

In the past, I would have asked Nora to check out Phorcys for me. Now, I didn't have a source of information about Mary's mysterious friend.

I knew a few people who supported Nora's agency, though. One was an old Army buddy named Aaron Sanchez. He could probably get answers to my questions about Phorcys.

I trusted Aaron more than anybody else I knew; the bond from our Army days was strong, even after all these years. He was loyal to me because of our old connection, though I wouldn't take that for granted.

I needed to test the waters with Aaron. I would buy a throwaway cellphone while I was in St. Martin. I could call Aaron at his office number. I would ask him to call me back; we couldn't talk freely until he was away from his government office.

3

"HELLO, IS ELENA HOWARD THERE?" I ASKED, WHEN MY CALL was answered by a man giving an extension number. I recognized Aaron's voice.

I was in a waterfront café on the Dutch side of St. Martin, having just finished breakfast. I made the first drawbridge opening and got *Island Girl* anchored on the Dutch side of the lagoon. Once I inflated the dinghy, I cleared in with Dutch customs. A block down Airport Road, I found a shop selling prepaid phones. And by then, I was starving for breakfast.

"Elena Howard? Nobody like that here. What number were you calling?"

"Sorry. I mis-dialed."

"Okay. No problem. I thought I rec — "

"Yeah, thanks," I mumbled. "I'm using a strange phone. Gotta look up the number. Try again."

"Sure. *Hasta luego*," he said.

Standing and picking up my check, I disconnected the

call and turned off the phone. With a fingernail, I popped the back off and removed the SIM card.

I put the phone and the SIM in my pocket and walked to the cash register. After paying for my meal, I crossed the street to another coffee shop. I took a table that gave me a view of the place I just left.

My phone call to Aaron was risky. He was a good guy; I've known him since we went through jump school at Fort Benning right after I got out of college. I didn't know what Nora might have told him and the rest of her troops about me, though.

We've done this before, Aaron and I. Elena Howard was a girl we knew back when we were young and foolish. Her name ensured that he would recognize my voice. From our brief exchange, he would know I was worried about being tracked.

He decoded my request for him to "get the number" I was calling from and "try again later." His "*Hasta luego*" comment told me he knew I wanted him to call me back. Despite his name, Aaron didn't normally lapse into Spanish without a reason. *Hasta luego* — until later — was a signal that he understood me. An eavesdropper would take it as a throw-away comment, but Aaron meant it literally.

When he called back, he would use a burner phone of his own. My worry was what might happen between now and then. My inbound call to his office number would have been logged automatically. Depending on how the algorithms were set up that day, it might have been flagged for a trace, or even recorded.

Once I got my coffee in the second café, I watched the entrance to the place across the road, the one where I ate breakfast and called Aaron. In the worst case, I would soon see the cops show up, looking for me. If Nora knew about my call to Aaron, it would only be a matter of a few minutes before they came.

If Aaron returned my call while my phone was off the network, he would leave a message. He wouldn't return the call if Nora set the hounds on my trail. Or if he did, he would call from his office phone. Seeing the caller ID from his office would tell me I needed to stay clear of him.

I left my coffee on the table long enough to go to the cash register and buy a newspaper. Then I settled in for a couple of hours of surveillance. After I finished the paper and several more cups of coffee, I decided the coast was clear. I put the SIM back in the phone and powered it on to discover a voicemail from an unknown number in the 703 area code — Northern Virginia.

That was from Aaron; his home and his office were both in Northern Virginia. I retrieved the voicemail. It was short and to the point.

"This is a clean number. Call me on it anytime outside office hours."

After I removed the SIM, I put the phone back in my pocket. Aaron at least thought he was clean, but I wasn't taking any chances.

I would spend the rest of the day taking care of my errands in St. Martin. Before I sailed for Puerto Rico that evening, I would call Aaron while I could get a cellphone signal. Once I was offshore, there would be no service.

4

ISLAND GIRL WAS ROLLING IN THE SWELL THAT WORKED ITS WAY around Pelican Point and into Simpson Bay. With the wind from the southeast, the anchorage was uncomfortable, but I wasn't planning to stay long. My business in St. Martin was wrapped up in time for me to make the last drawbridge opening out of the lagoon. I anchored just outside the channel to the drawbridge to make my cellphone calls.

I cleared out for departure with customs and immigration, declaring my destination as Fajardo, Puerto Rico. I put Fajardo on the paperwork to offer a little misdirection. I actually planned to clear into Puerto Rico at Culebra. If people with access to the customs databases were looking for me, they would be waiting in Fajardo.

When I didn't show up in a reasonable time, they would check inbound clearances for other ports. Then they would discover I was in Puerto Rico, but I would have a little head start on them. I wouldn't be in Culebra for long before I headed for Bahia Guánica, where I expected to meet Mary. There would be no paper trail after I cleared in at Culebra.

Mary was one reason I dropped the anchor after I came out from the lagoon. The other was my friend Aaron Sanchez. Once I was a few miles from St. Martin, I wouldn't have cellphone service, and I wanted to check in with both of them.

At *Island Girl's* chart table, I opened my laptop and went online using a satellite hotspot, one of my day's purchases. With the hotspot, I would have internet access even when far offshore. I logged on and navigated to the blind email drop Mary and I shared.

I left a message there for her before I departed from Miami the other day. That was a few minutes after I spoke with Nora via our dedicated encrypted satellite phones. I was shocked to hear from Nora then, after her "execution" in St. Thomas a few days earlier.

The crooked FBI agent I mentioned before — a man named George Kelley — ordered Nora's execution. He was there in the room with us when one of his minions killed a woman I thought was Nora.

Nora's faked execution in St. Thomas was supposed to intimidate me and get me to roll over on Mary. Seconds after Kelley and company killed the stand-in, Mary and I sprang our own trap and killed Kelley and two of his henchmen. We didn't know the identity of the woman who died in Nora's place.

Soon after that, I got a text about my daughter's kidnapping. My daughter shouldn't have been part of this. She didn't even know I existed, let alone that I was her father. Nobody but her mother and I knew.

Why that was so is a story for another time. The point was, these people found out and went after her, looking for leverage over me.

A quick call from Mary to her friend Phorcys resulted in my daughter's rescue and the deaths of the goons who were holding her. Through Phorcys, we learned who ordered the kidnapping.

Mary and I killed that person ourselves; I'm a vengeful bastard when it comes to threats to innocent people. Before he died, the son of a bitch told us how they learned about my daughter. It seems Nora, or as he called her, Phyllis Greer, told them.

I wasn't aware that she knew about my daughter, but she must have gotten access to my old Army records, where the story of my divorce was recorded. Those records were beyond Top Secret; they were hidden away when I joined the group Nora was running now.

Nora didn't know yet that I uncovered her duplicity; she was continuing her effort to manipulate me. She and her cronies were after Mary and the files, and they saw me as a means to their end.

Back to Mary. After we killed that man who arranged my daughter's kidnapping, we thought we should split up for a couple of weeks.

We were careful not to leave evidence, but the coincidence of our presence in the neighborhood of two hits wouldn't be overlooked. Kelley and our other victim were connected to each other; that would be enough to make Mary and me suspects.

We didn't want to be too easy to find. Mary stayed in the States, and I flew back to the BVI and picked up *Island Girl*. Back then, Mary and I were planning to meet two weeks later in Bahia Guánica, Puerto Rico.

When I sent my message to Mary the day before yesterday, I gave her enough hints about Nora so she had at least an idea of what was going on. I was changing my strategy from "run and hide" to "seek and destroy."

A two-week delay would just give Nora and company that much more time to find us. I asked Mary to meet me in Puerto Rico in two days instead of two weeks.

I was relieved when I found her answer in the email drop.

That's great news. Glad your old girlfriend survived. She may be able to tell us something useful. Can't wait to see you both.

That senator's suicide in Florida caused such a stir that I can't get anything done here, anyway. Headed your way day after tomorrow. I'll join you at our rendezvous the day after I arrive; getting in late, will stay near the airport and go to our place the next morning.

Don't reply — no time for me to check; in a hurry. I'll explain when I see you.

Love,

Mary.

That brought a smile to my face. I put the laptop away and took out the burner phone I used to call Aaron earlier.

5

"What's going on?" Aaron asked, answering my call.

"Got a few minutes?"

"For you, always. I haven't forgotten who saved my ass that time."

"This time, it's my ass on the line."

"Happy to help, man. Just ask."

"First thing, have you noticed anything strange about our boss lady?"

"You mean aside from the fact that she put out the word that you've gone rogue?"

"She said that?"

"Not in so many words, but the implication was clear enough."

"Any reactions to that from the rest of the agency?" I asked.

"No, but you know how compartmentalized we are. Good chance I wouldn't hear anything."

"What do you think about it?"

"You going rogue? Man, you shouldn't even need to ask.

You *know* what I think about it. She's wandered off the reservation. You got any idea what she's up to?"

"Yeah. She's been bought by the mob."

"The *mob*? I would have figured maybe the Chinese or the Russians got their hooks into her somehow. Or even some of the Arabs, maybe. But the *mob*? You sure about that?"

"As sure as I ever get about stuff like this." I gave Aaron a quick rundown on Mary's adventures, leaving out her identity, but emphasizing the files she stole. "And they found out about Abby. They kidnapped her to try to make me give them the girl and the files."

"Ah, shit, man. You know who took her?"

"Yeah. They've all paid for their sins already. She's home safe, none the wiser."

"But how could the boss even have known about Abby? Nobody but the guys on the team back then knew, and none of them would have..." His voice trailed off.

"What?" I asked.

"Just thinking about who might have told her. I guess there could be something about all that in your old 201 file, but I thought those were buried deep when we came over here."

"That's my guess, the 201. You in touch with any of the guys who were with us back then?"

"No. They all bought it on their next mission. That was after you moved over. My transfer was in process, so I wasn't with them that time. I was still in the loop, but I guess you weren't, by then."

"No. I'm sad to hear that."

"Yeah. We were a hell of a team. Back to now, though. You think the boss has the clout to get her hands on our 201s?"

"I don't know about her, but the guy she told about Abby was high enough up where he could have gotten my 201 for her. He could have gotten any kind of classified military records, if he knew what to ask for."

"You gonna ask him about it?"

"I already did, but I didn't probe that particular subject. Once I found out it was the boss who told him about Abby, he didn't have any reason to keep on living."

"Wait a minute. Are we talking about who I think we are?" Aaron asked.

"Maybe. Who are you thinking about?"

"A recent high-profile suicide with some embarrassing history. A senator."

"Could well be the same person."

"Nice work, buddy. How the hell did you find him?"

"That brings me to the reason for my call." I told him about Mary's friend, Phorcys.

"Sounds like a good person to have on your side."

"Maybe. But I'm not sure whose side he's on. Right now, it suits him to help my lady friend, but he doesn't owe *me* anything, and I'm not sure what his connection is to her."

"You sure you want to know? I mean, you said you were tight with her. You start digging into stuff like that, you might find shit you would rather not know."

"I'm willing to take that risk. I trust her. It's him I'm not sure about. He could be playing her. I doubt it, but I want to know who he is, anyway. You think you can help?"

"Hell, yes. You know damn well I can. You know any more about him than what you just told me?"

"No. You have everything."

"Okay, then. I got some work to do. Good to hear from you. Take care. I'll call when I get something. If you pick up any more hints about Phorcys, call me. Even small things can help."

"Thanks," I said.

"My pleasure," Aaron said, and he disconnected the call.

I put the phone and the laptop away and made sure everything below deck was secured for open water. After I turned on the navigation lights, I climbed up into the cockpit. Two minutes later, the anchor was lashed on the bow and I raised the main and my biggest headsail.

I trimmed the sails for a beam reach, and *Island Girl* accelerated to six knots in a few boat lengths. When I was out of Simpson Bay, I took up a course of 278 degrees magnetic and eased the sheets for a broad reach. That would put me off the southeast tip of Puerto Rico late the next afternoon.

6

I ANCHORED JUST INSIDE THE ENTRANCE TO ENSENADA HONDA in Culebra and took the dinghy into town. After clearing in with customs and immigration, I bought a cold six-pack and some minutes for my throwaway cellphone at a little store near the dinghy dock.

Back aboard *Island Girl*, I put my paperwork away and retrieved the burner cellphone and my laptop. Settling into the cockpit with a cold beer, I checked the email drop, just in case Mary's plans changed. There was no message from her, which was good news. She should arrive in Puerto Rico late tomorrow. I would see her in Bahia Guánica the day after.

That worked out well. I was a hundred-mile sail from there. I would leave Culebra this evening and get *Island Girl* situated in Bahia Guánica late tomorrow afternoon. I would have time to pick up a few groceries and clean the boat up from the voyage before Mary got there.

Before I sipped my beer, I turned on the burner cellphone. Once it acquired service, the voicemail indicator flashed. I thumbed my way through the menus and saw that

I missed a call from Aaron. It was a bit early in the day; he was probably in his office. I was surprised he didn't want me to wait until after working hours to call. I listened to the message, but he just said, "Call when you get this. Any time's good." Taking him at his word, I called.

"Hey. That you?" he said, when he answered.

"Yep. Who else?"

"Just checking. You got my message?"

"Yeah, all you said was call when I got it. You at work?"

"No. I left early so I could talk with you. I've got information on that person you asked about."

"Everything okay?" The part about leaving early so he could talk to me worried me.

"Yeah, no problem. I couldn't find your guy in our system, though. So I bought a late lunch for a friend who knows stuff that's not in the databases. She's heard of this Phorcys. Or at least somebody she thinks might be him. You where you can talk?"

"Yes. I'm all alone. Closest boat's anchored half a mile from me. Is your friend one of us?"

"No, she's not one of us. She's in the private sector. Works for a think tank. She's a researcher. We help one another out from time to time. Anyhow, about Phorcys. You said he was connected with a criminal organization?"

"I don't know that; I'm guessing." I thought about Phorcys wiping out the people who snatched Abby. But who was I to judge him a criminal? "Why do you ask?"

"Because that part doesn't fit. My friend says there are rumors about somebody who uses the name Phorcys, but nobody thinks he's a criminal."

"You're losing me," I said.

"She and her sources think Phorcys is a pseudonym used

by a reclusive billionaire who funds a lot of moderate politicians. He's nonpartisan, but he doesn't like extremists of any kind — conservative or liberal. You with me so far?"

"Yeah, but who is he?"

"Nobody knows. Whoever he is, he hides behind a lot of shell companies. And he backs middle-of-the-road, straight-arrow politicians."

"But he's not a crook?"

"Not that anybody knows, anyway. But she did say he makes his own rules, whoever he is. Nobody has ever connected him with anything criminal."

"And why does she think this unknown guy might be Phorcys? I'm not following the logic, here."

"Yeah. It's tenuous, all right. The behavior pattern you described fits the man they call Phorcys."

"Behavior pattern?" I asked. "How much did you tell her?"

"Nothing that will come back on any of us. I sketched out the story about you and your lady friend, but I left out the bad parts. Mostly, my source focused on the phone calls you mentioned. I told her you stumbled over files that might implicate several prominent politicians in corrupt activity, and that they tried to strong-arm you into giving up the files. The part about them kidnapping an innocent person for leverage got her hooked. When she found out your friend called Phorcys for help, she got excited. That's the kind of thing this guy does; they look at him as a knight in shining armor. He's always doing good. Never sets a foot wrong, according to her."

I thought about the people who died in retribution for Abby's kidnapping and shook my head. Aaron didn't know those details, so he couldn't have shared them with his friend.

"If it's the same guy, your friend's only seen part of the picture," I said.

"That's probably so. Anyhow, that's all I have so far. She thought the Florida connection matched up with the Phorcys they know, though. Especially his in-depth knowledge of everything that happens there, legal or not. She's going to do a little more snooping and get back to me."

"Okay. Thanks," I said.

"No problem. One more thing I need to ask you before we hang up."

"Sure. What's that?"

"I think I know the answer, but I told her I'd ask, okay?"

"Okay. What's she want?"

"To talk with your lady friend, basically. How does she know Phorcys? What's her connection to him? Any chance she might talk to my friend? None of that's meant as a quid pro quo, but... Well, she wanted me to ask."

"I understand. I have no clue about her relationship with Phorcys. And she's not likely to talk with anybody about anything. Like I said when we spoke before, she's one of us, just working in the private sector. Sorry."

"No need to apologize. I understand. I'll call when I have more."

"Thanks, man. Stay safe."

"Yeah. You, too." With that, Aaron disconnected.

Picking up my beer, I found it was warm. I needed to move on, anyway. Pouring the beer over the side, I cranked the diesel and went up to the bow to retrieve the anchor. I wanted to get out of the Ensenada Honda entrance channel while there was enough light to see the reefs.

7

THE ENTRANCE TO BAHIA GUÁNICA MADE ME NERVOUS. IT WAS buoyed and straight-forward, but there were unmarked reefs to the west of the channel. Late in the day they were hard to see, and there was often a strong current sweeping across the channel. It would only take a moment of inattention to end up wrecked on the submerged coral.

Once I was northwest of the little mangrove island called Gilligan's Island, I relaxed. Out of the current, I had a straight shot into the bay's entrance. The opening between two steep hills looked like a misplaced fjord. I started the diesel; the high ground on either side of the entrance would soon block the wind.

Safely in the protected water of the entrance, I lashed the tiller and throttled back to crawl speed. I went forward and dropped the sails; I would have to motor into my chosen anchorage.

When I reached the north end of the marked channel leading to the town of Guánica, I turned about 45 degrees to port. Guánica itself was a good-sized town, but a mile to the west was a relatively secluded spot in a cove called Cueva de la Julia.

Close enough to the main town for easy dinghy access, it was a quiet, well-protected anchorage. There were two unoccupied local boats on moorings, but otherwise, *Island Girl* and I had it to ourselves.

Once satisfied that the anchor was holding, I went below. I spent half an hour putting the boat in order and then took a beer out of the icebox. Exhausted from three overnight sails in a row, I decided to skip going into town.

There was plenty of food aboard for a day or two. Mary was planning to stay near the airport in San Juan tonight, since she was arriving late. She would take a bus to Guánica in the morning, and we could do our grocery shopping there when I took the dinghy in to meet her.

From the drawer below the chart table, I retrieved my iPhone and the burner phone I was using to communicate with Aaron Sanchez. I settled myself in the cockpit and turned both phones on before I popped the top on my beer.

After my first sip, the phones were up and running. No one had called the iPhone; that was what I expected. Aaron had left a voicemail on the burner, though. Thinking he must have learned more about Phorcys, I retrieved the message.

"Call me as soon as you can. Shit's happening." The message was less than an hour old.

I took another swallow of beer and returned his call.

"You get my message?" he asked by way of a greeting.

"Yeah. Shit's happening?"

"Yep. Looks like the boss wants me out. I had a visit from humanoid resources right after lunch. They're 'downsizing,' as they say, 'consolidating my function with another department in furtherance of our mission and for greater synergy.' Their bullshit words."

"So do you have any options?"

"Not really. There's a sweetener if I waive a bunch of appeals I'm entitled to and sign a non-disclosure agreement. Otherwise, I only get my retirement." He chuckled.

"A non-disclosure agreement?"

"Yeah. Like they don't already have that covered."

"Are more people being let go?" I asked.

"Not that I know of, but I don't have good intel on that. That's why I called, though. Something's rotten here. I got a firm indication that you were right about our boss — former boss, that is."

"You mean about her being dirty?"

"Yeah, but not exactly on that point. You got me to thinking yesterday when we talked about those 201 files. I followed up on that. On mine, specifically."

"Just yours? Not mine?"

"Yeah. When I checked yesterday, there was no record of yours."

"That's what I would have expected. But what about yours?"

"My source found mine, all right. It was filed in a special place, well-hidden — wouldn't have been found by anyone who didn't already know a lot about my service. That was yesterday, in the morning. They were going to do an access audit when they couldn't find yours, based on my telling them yours should be there if mine was. My source was puzzled by that, too; said it couldn't happen. He agreed with me, said if mine was there, yours should have been."

"Okay," I said. "And?"

"And my source got back to me later in the day yesterday.

My 201 was pulled by someone up the line from me between the time I spoke to my source and the time he called me back. You know who's up the line from me, right?"

"Same as with me. The boss lady, whoever that undersecretary is that she reports to, and then — "

"Yeah," Aaron interrupted. "Don't even say it out loud, man. I don't know how, but they gotta know I was checking stuff for you. Maybe I got a microchip implanted in my ass or something. Or you do."

"You're reading too much sci-fi. The boss probably pulled my 201 to see who I might be connected with from way back when. When she went looking to see who was in our unit, there you were."

"Maybe. But I'm not sure how she could have done that. Doesn't really matter. My source called again this morning, right before the visit from HR. That audit deal I mentioned? Turns out they ran it, and this time there was no trace of either of our 201s being accessed."

"But wait," I said. "Your source — "

"Yeah. Saw my damn file with his own eyes yesterday. Saw the digital sign-out for it yesterday afternoon, too. Guess he was hallucinating, because there never was such a file. Now we're both in limbo, you and me."

"Shit," I said. "I'm sorry I got you into this."

"No, man. I owe you my life. And I'm not through with these assholes yet. I'm just getting started. They've pissed me off, now."

"But you're out, right? You took their deal?"

"Yeah, sure. I took their deal. I'm angry, not stupid. Live to fight another day. Now I'm takin' the gloves off and goin' after them. They're gonna think they're surrounded before I get through with 'em."

"What are you going to do?"

"I'm goin' in business with a few friends. You need intel now more than ever, man. You know they got their sights on you and your lady. If you need to know shit, just ask me. Same as always."

"But how will you get access to their data?" I asked.

Aaron laughed. "It's not *their* data. It's just data. They only *think* it's theirs. Anything I could get before, I can get now. My friends and I, we help one another out, just like you and I always have. We trust each other — not the damn bureaucrats. I'm still working on the Phorcys thing. I'll be in touch tomorrow on that, probably, but expect me to call from a different number. This one's gonna be history as soon as we hang up."

"Thanks," I said. "If you need anything from me, let me know."

"Yeah, man. Stay cool. Talk with you tomorrow."

8

"HEY, SAILOR! YOU IN PAIN?"

I was wide awake the instant I heard her voice. It was one in the morning when the iPhone woke me, and I groaned when I answered it.

"Hey, yourself. What time is it?"

"One o'clock. What was that groan for?"

"Just my excitement bubbling over. Your flight just get in?"

"I'm at the hotel. Sorry if I woke you, but I couldn't resist hearing your voice."

"Mm. I know what you mean. Glad we didn't end up waiting two weeks. What time do you figure on getting to Guánica?"

"The shuttle's picking me up at 6:30. Look for me around nine. Where's a good place to meet?"

"The waterfront; there are a few little fishing boats on moorings. *Island Girl's* about a mile to the west. So far, we've got this little cove to ourselves."

"Good. Sounds perfect for what I have in mind."

"Oh?" I asked. "What's that?"

"You'll see. Now go back to sleep. You're going to need your rest."

"Wait. You have any news?"

"Yes. But not now, okay? It'll take a while to tell you, and I'm beat from the trip. It's nothing that won't keep, anyway."

"Okay. Glad you're here."

"Me, too. Can't wait to see you."

With that, she was gone, and I was wide awake. My body clock was out of whack after three days of round-the-clock sailing, snatching 10-to-15-minute naps when I could. After five hours of sleep, I was ready to go — except there was nothing for me to do at this time of night.

Rather than lie in bed and fret, I got up and went up into the cockpit. It was deathly quiet outside except for the occasional pop of a fish striking some hapless insect on the water's surface.

The moon was new. There wasn't much moonlight, but the lights from the houses along the south shore of the cove cast a dim glow over the water. I could see occasional ripples on the glassy surface from feeding fish. The north shore was mostly parkland; it was dark in that direction.

I wondered what news Mary would have, and that reminded me that Aaron expected to have information about Phorcys tomorrow. I should have warned him that I would have company; I wasn't ready to tell Mary I was investigating her friend. She might be offended by that.

Or maybe she wouldn't; after all, it was the kind of thing people like us did. Trust didn't come easily to people in our line of work; staying alive required constant vigilance. And that made me wonder what Mary's news might be.

We discovered a few days ago that someone was trying to

fill the power vacuum left when Mary killed a mobster named Rory O'Hanlon. O'Hanlon was Mary's client; he hired her to kill his money guy, who was skimming while laundering O'Hanlon's illicit cash.

Part of her job was to recover the files that were the root of our problems. The guy who was skimming maintained the files; he was like O'Hanlon's chief financial officer. F.X. Dailey was his name; his wife was in it with him.

Mary followed through on her contract with O'Hanlon, but he thought she knew too much about his business and tried to kill her instead of paying her. That didn't end well for him, and Mary kept the files. But that wasn't the news; it was background.

When I met Mary, O'Hanlon was trying to retrieve the files and do away with her. At that stage, we thought the files contained lists of his suppliers and distributors. Since then, we learned that the files included lists of corrupt politicians. Now we knew that O'Hanlon was only a cog in an extensive, corrupt enterprise that reached the highest levels of our government.

When my daughter was kidnapped to force me to give up Mary and the files, Mary and I tracked down the man who ordered the kidnapping. We interrogated him before we helped him commit suicide.

We learned two things from him. One was that the person who told him to go after us was taking over O'Hanlon's empire. The man we questioned didn't know more about him than that. He never saw the mystery man. He met the mystery man once, but was blindfolded for the encounter. After that, he took orders over the phone. The mystery man's voice was distinctive, perhaps with a slight accent.

The second, and to me, the more disturbing thing we learned, was that my boss told them about my daughter. My daughter was born while I was in the Army. I was out of the country, serving in one of those places the government won't talk about. I was officially missing in action for over a year. Before I even knew about my daughter, her mother divorced me and remarried. Her new husband adopted the girl, and they lived normal lives.

I kept my distance, for several reasons. One of them was the fear of exactly this kind of thing. My boss shouldn't have even known about my daughter; that whole part of my life was buried in ultra-secret files from my military days. As Aaron Sanchez discovered, the corruption in our government reached levels that had access even to files like mine and his.

While Mary was killing time in the States, she was going to try to find out more about the mystery man. We agreed that I would focus on how my boss discovered the existence of my daughter. My other task was to find someone who could crack the encryption that protected the files Mary acquired from O'Hanlon.

By now, Aaron and I knew as much as we were ever likely to learn about how my daughter's existence was disclosed. But I still needed to talk with him about decrypting the files. That was something Aaron would farm out to one of his "friends." His abrupt termination wouldn't stop us from that, but it might slow us down.

I would call him in the morning before Mary got here. I could explain the delicacy of the Phorcys research and discuss the decryption of the files at the same time. Then I would have progress to report to Mary.

And now I was sleepy again. Not wanting to know how

late it was, I went below and crawled into my berth without looking at the clock. Soon, I would be with Mary again, and we could sort all this out.

9

THE SUN STREAMING IN THROUGH THE PORTLIGHT OVER MY berth woke me up; a glance at the clock on the bulkhead told me it was a few minutes before 6 o'clock. I went in the head and splashed water on my face. Then I put a pot of coffee on the stove.

Given the one-hour time difference, it was too early to call Aaron. And he said he was ditching his burner phone. I couldn't call him anyway, until he gave me a new number.

That made me think I should replace my burner phone; I could do that here while I was waiting on Mary. The notion of buying disposable phones made me chuckle.

I remember when cellphones were horrendously expensive. But $25 cellphones that came with $15 worth of talk-time were available everywhere, now.

As I waited for the coffee to perk, I got out my laptop and the burner phone. I plugged the phone in to charge, and when the screen lit up, I saw the indicator for a new text message.

Unlocking the phone, I scrolled through the menu and

found a message from a strange number in the 301 area code. The message was short. "Using this, now." That would be Aaron's new number, a Maryland number instead of another Virginia one. He was being extra careful.

Looking at the clock, I decided if I waited an hour, I could find somewhere in Guánica to buy another throwaway phone. That way, I could call him from a new number, further reducing the chance of our exposure to Nora's spies.

I poured a cup of coffee and took the laptop up into the cockpit. Getting lucky, I found an open Wi-Fi network from a bar in Guyapao Barrio, which was close to the west end of the cove. I could have used my satellite hotspot, but Wi-Fi was faster. Using my VPN, I set up a free cloud storage account and uploaded the encrypted files that the crooks wanted so badly.

I would share the login credentials for the cloud account with Aaron later in the morning. He could download the file and then close the account. It wasn't the most secure arrangement, but it wasn't too bad, and the files were encrypted to begin with. Besides, the files would only be there for an hour or two.

The upload took several minutes. Leaving the laptop running in the cockpit, I shaved and got dressed. By the time I finished my coffee and scarfed down a quick breakfast, the upload was done. I put the computer in my canvas briefcase.

It was a little after 7 o'clock. Inflating the dinghy, launching it, and mounting the outboard took another 20 minutes. By the time I got ashore, it would be 8 o'clock, and the stores in town should be open. I locked *Island Girl*, leaving a short length of transparent monofilament fishing line caught between two of the drop boards in the companionway.

If anybody came aboard in my absence, I would be able to tell. They couldn't get below without moving that scrap of line. Even if they were careful enough to notice it, they wouldn't get it back in exactly the same place.

It was a few minutes after eight when I locked the dinghy to the seawall along the boardwalk in Guánica. I climbed out and ambled around town until I found one of those stores that are ubiquitous in the Caribbean. It sold a bit of everything from clothing to groceries to building supplies. And prepaid cellphones.

With my new phone and a foam-plastic cup of sour coffee, I walked back to where I left the dinghy. There were park benches looking out over the water. Surprised there were no people hanging out there, I sat down and called Aaron.

"Yeah?" he answered, not recognizing my new number.

"Is Elena there?" I asked.

"Elena? Elena who?"

"Elena Howard."

"Okay. I see you got my message."

"Yeah. Figured it was time I got a new phone, too."

"Good for you. Glad you did. Can't be too careful. But I don't have anything for you yet. It'll be later today."

"That's okay. That's why I'm calling; I'll have company here in about an hour, so I won't be able to talk about Phorcys."

"Company, huh? Your friend? The one who knows him?"

"Yeah. That one. I don't want her to know we're checking up on him. Not just yet, anyway. This phone will be turned off while she's around."

"Can't say as I blame you. Want me to just leave you a voicemail?"

"Sure. Or a text. But I've got something else to ask you."

"No problem, man. What do you need?"

"Those files I mentioned..."

"Yeah, I remember. What about them?"

"The names are encrypted. You got somebody who can help?"

"Damn right. How's the best way for me to get the files?"

"Write down this web address." I rattled off the URL of the cloud storage service.

"Got it. User name and password?"

I gave him those, and he read them back. "Once you download the files, erase them from the cloud and close the account, okay?"

"You got it. Not sure how long this'll take, but I'll be in touch later today on the mystery man thing. I'll have a better idea on the files then. Enjoy your guest, and take care, man."

"Thanks. I'll owe you."

"No way. Later."

"Hey," I said, "can we talk about something else?"

"Yeah, sure. I didn't mean to cut you off."

"You didn't cut me off, but given your situation, and mine, I think we should quit using the phones, unless it's an emergency."

"Okay, but how do you want to communicate, then?"

"I'll set up an email account on a secure server and share the login credentials with you. You can access it over a VPN. It'll work like a virtual blind drop. I'll leave a message for you in the drafts folder. When you get it, delete it and leave your response in the drafts folder. I'll delete it when I've read it. We'll each check it as often as we can."

"Cool. That's way better than the burner phones, as far as security."

"Yeah, and besides that, I bought myself a satellite hotspot. Now I can go online when I'm out of sight of land — out of cellphone range. Check email, do a little online research, whatever."

"Okay. That's great. Just let me know how to work the email drop, okay? Guess I'll just need the email address and the password?"

"Yep. And the web address for online access to the server. I'll send it all in a coded text."

"Okay. You gonna send a key for the code? Like separately? That's what I recommend."

"No," I said, remembering how Mary set up the blind drop she and I were using. "Nobody but you will figure out what the text means. It may take you a couple of tries, but I doubt it. Just think about the shit we did when we got leave way back when. It'll fall into place."

"Okay, then. I'll look for it. Stay safe."

"Yeah. You too. It'll take me a little while to put it together. Probably about an hour. Thanks again."

"Sure, man." Aaron disconnected the call, and I powered my new burner phone off and put it in my canvas briefcase with the laptop. I sipped my coffee and watched the colorful little outboard-powered fishing boats bobbing on their moorings.

It was almost 9 o'clock. Mary would be here in a few minutes. I got busy and set up the blind email drop for Aaron and sent him a text with the information he would need to access it.

10

I WAS FINISHING MY COFFEE AND WATCHING A TWO-FOOT-LONG iguana sunning itself on the edge of the seawall when the shuttle van stopped near the little gazebo. By the time I got to the gazebo, the driver was opening the side door. Mary, her backpack on one shoulder, stepped down and handed him some folded bills. She grinned, throwing her arms wide for my hug.

"Thank you, ma'am," the driver said, closing the door and pocketing the money. "Enjoy your holiday."

She was still in my arms when the shuttle drove away.

"I've missed you," I said.

"I missed you, too."

"Had breakfast yet?" I asked.

"No, just coffee. But I'm okay. A snack would be good, though, unless you're in a hurry to get to the boat."

"I thought we could pick up a few groceries. I haven't stocked the galley since I got back."

"Really? What have you been doing all this time?"

"Sailing. I've been to St. Martin and back."

"That's a lot of miles in three days. When did you get here?"

"Last night. First full night's sleep I've had in days."

"What took you to St. Martin?"

"There's a hole-in-the-wall place there that sells exotic electronics. I had a little shopping to do."

We were walking and talking; Mary pulled me to a stop at an open-air café. She led me to the counter and ordered coffee and a fried saltfish patty. I settled for coffee, sure it would be better than the swill I got from the convenience store earlier. Mary set her food on a table and dropped her backpack in one of the extra chairs.

"What kind of electronics?"

"Security scanning stuff — to detect bugs, spy cameras, tracking devices. Plus a sackful of spy stuff for us to use if we want. And a satellite hotspot, so we have internet access anytime, anywhere."

She nodded. "Any special reason for all the spy stuff?"

"Well, after your friends planted that tracker on the boat right after we met, I thought it might be a good idea. We're up against the professionals, now, too. Not just regular crooks."

"What do you mean, 'professionals?'"

"I told you Nora was alive."

"Yes, but that's about it. What's going on?"

"She called me when I was about to board my flight in Miami. Spun me a yarn about how the whole Kelley thing was a setup."

"No shit. Tell me about it."

"She tried to convince me that 'they' — that would be her team, they're the good guys, of course — were planning to record Kelley trying to force me to hand over you and the files. Then they were going to bust him, try to get him to flip on somebody higher up."

"What did you say to that?"

"I played along. At that point, she didn't know about the senator's suicide, so she thought I was in the dark about her betrayal."

Mary took a bite of her saltfish patty and nodded. "She called you on that dedicated sat phone?"

"Yes. After that, I sanitized it and got rid of it before I left Miami."

"Who was that woman they killed, then?" she asked.

"I don't know. Nora said she was going to die anyway — Kelley planned to kill her for some other reason, so they just used her."

"But you recognized her voice when she spoke to you in that hotel room; you said she was Nora."

"Yes. Nora was in an adjacent room with a transmitter. They had a receiver and a speaker in the bag that was over the woman's head. So I heard Nora's voice, thought it was coming from the woman."

Mary frowned and shook her head. "They wasted her as part of a ruse. Bastards. I'm glad I killed the three of them. Wish I could have shot your friend Nora, in the bargain."

"Hold that thought. We'll get to her before this is over, but there's more."

"Did you find somebody who could decrypt the files?"

"I sent them off this morning; no news on that yet. There was a small distraction." I told Mary about my conversations with Aaron Sanchez, leaving out the part about Phorcys.

"She told them *you* had gone rogue?"

"It doesn't surprise me. Aaron couldn't tell me how the

others reacted. They're compartmentalized. That makes it tough for rumors to circulate."

"If the organization's so compartmentalized, how do you know this Aaron person?"

"Years ago, she got him to call me and give me a briefing on a target. I recognized his voice. We go way back, to before either of us joined Nora's agency."

"Way back? You trust him?"

"Yeah. Aaron and I were in the Army together, in the same unit. We were part of a 12-person team that was sent into a certain Middle-Eastern country 22 years ago. The whole thing was super-secret. It's still under wraps."

"Was that when you were missing in action? When your wife divorced you?"

"Yes. I was listed as missing in action in a different country; that was part of the cover for our mission. Aaron was our intelligence officer, and my second in command. He was captured by the local secret police while he was working a source."

"And he escaped?"

"Yes. With a little help."

"Your help? You saved him?"

"So he says. I just did what I do; I killed a few bad people."

"How did you go from there to Nora's group?"

"Back then, it wasn't yet Nora's group. But the person running it recruited me. My job didn't change much, but the working conditions were better."

"Better how?"

"I could live like a normal human; sleep indoors in a bed, eat regular food. Didn't have to worry as much about getting my throat cut in the desert. That kind of thing."

"And they recruited your friend Aaron, too?"

"Yes. We were out of touch for years, until that telephone briefing. We didn't get much chance to compare notes until the last few days. When we talked before, it was strictly mission-focused. Neither of us let anybody else know we knew one another. We could slip in a few references to shared experiences every so often, but that was the extent of our conversations."

"What changed?"

"I called him to see if he knew any more about Nora."

"I'm fascinated, Finn. This is like spy-movie stuff." Mary nudged my leg under the table and winked. "So, what did he say?"

"About Nora? Only that she put out the word that I was a rogue agent. He knew that was horse shit. I asked him if he could find out how she learned about Abby. He knew about that whole situation from when we were deployed together."

"And?"

"And as best we could tell before he got fired, somebody got my Army records, which were supposed to be off limits to everybody but God."

"Aaron got fired?"

"It's a long story. Short version is somebody got wind of his request and both of our files from back then disappeared, like they never existed."

"But how could he do that, anyway? Get his hands on the files, I mean."

"It's what Aaron does. He knows people, cultivates relationships. A buddy of his worked in the department that handles the security for records like those. Somebody who owed him a favor."

"Another member of your Army unit?"

"No. Aaron told me all those people died on a mission right after he was transferred to what's now Nora's team."

"All they did was fire him? I'm surprised they let him out alive."

"Oh, they gave him an attractive retirement package."

"Why would they do that, Finn? It doesn't make sense. You two could bring them all down."

"Which is exactly why they did it. They're trying to give him a false sense of security. They got their hands on our old military records and discovered the connection between us. They already knew I asked him how they found out about my daughter. They figure he'll lead them to me. Then they'll kill us both."

"You're not talking to him anymore, are you?"

"Sure. Aaron and I are better at this than they are. We're both experienced field operatives. We're up against a bunch of desk jockeys like Nora. Black-hearted and evil, but they never broke a fingernail, let alone anybody's bones. Aaron's lining up somebody to decrypt the files right now. And he's the one I call when I need information about almost anything."

"But he must have been cut off from their data sources."

"I asked him about that. Seems that they're *his* sources. As Aaron put it, all that information is just data, sitting there. It's not *their* data. It's there for the taking, if you know where to look and who to ask."

"Where are you going with this whole Nora thing, Finn?"

"I'm going to kill her. I haven't worked out the details yet, and I want to make sure we get as much information out of her and her cronies as we can. But once I've done that, she'll die."

"I'm in."

"I know that. Thanks. You said you had news, too. Your turn."

"Let's get our groceries and go back to the boat. We need the laptop; I've got stuff on a thumb drive. It'll go faster if we can look at it while we talk. Besides, I've missed you; we need some private time."

"Yes, ma'am. Groceries and *Island Girl*, coming up."

11

I TIED THE DINGHY TO *ISLAND GIRL'S* MIDSHIP CLEAT AND climbed aboard. Mary sat in the dinghy and passed the bags of groceries up to me. I plopped them down on the side deck.

Taking the last bags she gave me back to the cockpit, I examined the drop boards before I unlocked the companionway. My telltale piece of monofilament line was gone. Someone came aboard while I was in Guánica.

I put the groceries down and turned to intercept Mary. By then, she was on the side deck, picking up two of the bags we piled there. Taking them from her, I set them on the coachroof and put my arms around her.

"Welcome home," I said, as she melted into my hug.

"Mm, I've missed you," she said, her head on my shoulder.

I put my lips close to her ear and whispered, "I've missed you, too. But somebody's been aboard since I left. Don't say anything you wouldn't want them to overhear, okay?"

She nodded and spoke in a normal tone. "Let's get this stuff put away, then we can celebrate our reunion."

"Okay." I kept my voice low. "Entertain yourself in the cockpit until I clear the area below. Sort the groceries, or something."

She nodded and gave me another kiss.

Taking a step back, I retrieved the two bags of groceries from the coachroof. I took them back to the cockpit, putting them next to the ones I left there a minute before. Leaving Mary to bring the rest of our groceries back, I put my key in the padlock and opened the companionway, setting the drop boards in the cockpit.

After a quick look around below deck, I could tell whoever boarded *Island Girl* searched her. They were good; there weren't any obvious signs of things being disturbed, but I left a few items deliberately out of place — things that I remembered to check. A folded shirt that wasn't quite aligned with the rest in the stack, that kind of thing. Nothing was out of place. They put things back more neatly than I left them. That gave them away.

Since I took the laptop and my phones ashore with me, there wasn't much for them to find. I opened the lid of the chart table and took out the stack of paper nautical charts, setting them aside. Far in the back of the chart storage area, there was a ten-inch-square opening in the bottom. It was concealed by a carefully matched piece of plywood, which I levered up with a fingernail.

Everything I kept in the hidden compartment — mostly the new electronics — was intact. I took out my bug detector and went over the entire area below deck, checking for listening devices or video cameras. Finding none, I picked up another scanner designed to spot GPS tracking devices. I got a hit against the underside of the coachroof, just forward of the mast.

"Okay," I called. "Come on down."

"Find anything?" Mary asked, as she backed down the companionway ladder.

"Yes. A GPS tracker. No audio or video bugs. We're probably clean that way, but I'll check above deck later, just to be sure. Meanwhile, we'll just speak softly down here. Don't say anything private on deck until I clear it."

"You think they would bug the outside and not the inside?"

"Better safe than sorry," I said, shrugging. "Probably not. But they're likely to be watching us, too. If they are, a parabolic mike wouldn't be a big surprise."

"Why do you think they're watching us?"

"The boat was clean when I brought her in last night. I didn't go ashore until this morning, so they searched her and put the tracker on while I was in Guánica. These people were good; they would have had a lookout ashore to warn the boarding party if I started to come back."

"But you can't see *Island Girl* from town. That point of land is in the way."

"Right. But they could have a lookout anywhere along the shoreline of the cove. That's park land to the north of us; it's public."

She nodded. "What did you ever do with the tracker Frankie's people put aboard when we were in Bequia, anyway? You mentioned it earlier."

"Stuck it on a random charter boat in St. Martin the other day when I was there."

She chuckled. "So they know you were there."

"If anybody's still tracking that one. There's a good chance everybody who knew about it is dead."

She smiled. "We can hope. How about your friend Nora? Think she knew?"

"Maybe. I figure she was a step or two removed from Frankie and O'Hanlon, though, so maybe not. It's possible Kelley told her about it. I'm not sure why she would have cared, though. Back then, she could track me using that special satellite phone she gave me. But that's why I put that tracker on the charter boat. Just in case somebody's watching it. Never miss a chance to confuse the enemy."

"What do you think we should do about this one?"

"The tracker? I don't know. They already know we're here, so it doesn't matter until we leave Bahia Guánica. I think we should take our time deciding what to do with it. You haven't told me your news, yet. Or your plans."

"No, I need to do that. But there's something else that's more compelling right now."

"What's that?"

"You sure they can't hear us, or see what we're doing?"

"Not below deck, they can't. Why?"

"I'll show you," she said, giving me a steamy look as she sauntered into the forward cabin. "Come with me, sailor."

"Is there any way I can persuade you to keep the fire burning for a little longer?" I asked.

"What?" Her look changed from steamy to stormy.

"You're making it tough, but we need to haul ass out of here, Mary."

The stormy look faded into a frown. "Why? This seems like such a peaceful spot."

"Yes, except we know we have company here, remember?

Whoever planted the tracker probably saw me meet you in town."

"You think they might come after us? Here?"

"Yes. If we give them time to assemble a team. And I don't like this spot, given that they know we're aboard. We're surrounded by land. It would be easy for somebody to sneak up on us."

"Well, shit! You really know how to take the wind out of a girl's sails, Finn."

"You can't imagine how sorry I am. I — "

"No. It's okay. I know you're right. Let's get moving. Take a rain check?"

"You bet. Once we're offshore..."

12

Twenty minutes later, we were motoring out of the Bahia Guánica channel. Mary raised the sails while the headlands were blocking the wind. She sheeted them in to keep them from flogging and sat down beside me.

"Thanks for humoring me," I said.

She smiled. "Thanks for not being blinded by lust like some people we know."

"It wasn't easy to pass up your offer, lady. Thanks for being good-natured about it. I'm just trying to make sure I have you around for a long time."

"It's not just me. You're on their hit list, too."

"Oh, sure. I know way too much, so they're going to try to nail me. Not until I lead them to Aaron, though. Or vice versa. But there's no reason for them to wait to grab you. They were probably figuring on trailing me until I connected with you," I said.

She smiled and nodded. "You could be right."

"You know I am. What they're really after is you and your files, remember? I'm just bait, for now. They might figure on knocking me out and taking you — come after me and Aaron later. You're their big problem. We don't want to hang around in places where they might be tempted to snatch you. That's why I wanted to get moving before they get their act together."

"Right," she said. "But now you've got me worried, too. There's still the tracker. Just leaving's not enough; they can follow us. Unless you're thinking of getting rid of it."

"Not getting rid of it, no."

"But why not? Why keep it aboard?"

"At some point, we may want them to find us. We can use it to lead them into a trap where we'll have the upper hand."

"But if we leave it alone, they could pick us off anytime," she said.

"I'm not planning to leave it alone."

"You've lost me, Finn."

I grinned. "I'm thinking of diddling with it."

"What?"

"Using some of the exotic electronic gear I bought." I waved my hands and wiggled my fingers, like a magician about to pull a coin from thin air. "I can scramble the tracker's little brain, make it tell them whatever we want."

"You're serious?"

"Absolutely."

"Wow! Cool! But Finn?"

"What?"

"I'm game, but where will we go?"

"We'll check out some of those uninhabited islands you wanted to see."

"What about reprogramming the tracker? When?"

"Soon. After we're far enough out so we don't raise their suspicions, in case they're watching."

"I'm glad to be back with you, Finn."

"And I'm glad you're back."

We were about to clear the headlands; I could feel the wind picking up.

"Take the tiller while I ease the sheets?" I asked.

We traded places, and I gradually let out the sheets as the sails filled. In a minute or two, I bent down to the instrument panel and shut off the diesel.

"That's better. It's nice to be sailing again," she said.

"One of the best parts of living like this," I said.

"Not to nag, but where *are* you taking me, skipper?"

"Have you done any research on those uninhabited islands?" I asked, with a smile. "Got one in mind?"

"No. No time for that until now. I'm at your mercy. You must have somewhere you're thinking about."

"Yep. Isla de Aves."

"Bird Island. Where is it?"

"Around 240 miles east-southeast. Maybe 150 miles west of the northern Leewards. Sits out there all by itself."

"How big is it?"

"Not very big. A few hundred yards long. Less than 100 yards wide. Got some big reefs out to the east, to break the swell. The highest point's maybe 10 or 12 feet above sea level. It's just big enough to have a decent anchorage on the west side."

"There's nothing there?"

"Birds. And the ruins of a marine science laboratory from the '70s, maybe."

"Maybe?"

"Not sure what the last season's storms may have done to it."

"Whose laboratory was it?"

"Venezuela's. They own the island, more or less."

"More or less?"

"Oh, the ownership's been contested over the years. I'm not sure where it stands, right now. The island itself isn't worth arguing about, except that it would expand the territorial waters of whatever country it belongs to. And there may be oil and gas under the seabed in the area."

"Does Venezuela patrol it, or anything? Will we have to clear in?"

"In theory, we should get permission from the Venezuelan Navy to go there. But given the present situation in Venezuela, I don't think they're likely to know or care. If they show up, they'll probably give us a little grief, but nothing that cold hard cash won't fix. Or maybe cold beers, depending on who's in charge. But I doubt we'll see anybody, Navy or otherwise."

"You've been there?"

"Yes, once. Just out of curiosity."

"Anything interesting?"

"No, not really, unless you're a serious bird-watcher."

"Sounds perfect. Just what I had in mind."

She was quiet for several seconds, watching two seagulls swooping along in the slipstream from our sails.

"And what are you going to tell the tracker to report?" she asked, when the birds left.

"I thought the Bahamas. Maybe the Out Islands. There are lots of uninhabited islands there, too. Most of them, in fact. We can keep those people busy chasing phantoms for a good while up there. And the best part is that it's the opposite way from where we're going — maybe 500 miles in the wrong direction."

"So, by the time they figure out what's happening, we'll be far, far away," Mary said, grinning.

"That's the plan."

"I like it. How long will it take you to 'diddle' it?"

"I don't know. I should probably go get started; I've got to cope with a learning curve. By the time I figure out what I'm doing, we should be far enough out. You okay to steer for a while? Just keep us headed roughly south, for now."

"Sure. Once you finish, I'll cook us some supper."

13

Sitting at the chart table, I studied the thick manual for the GPS spoofing device. The setup was more complicated than I expected. I plotted a route with latitude and longitude waypoints. By running a simulation at a specified boat speed using the navigation software in my laptop, I generated a data set that included waypoints and time/date stamps. I uploaded that data to the spoofer device.

Once that was done, the rest was simple enough. I needed to find the tracker and put the spoofer as close to it as possible. The tracker had an internal timer. Every 30 minutes, it would wake up, acquire a GPS position, and broadcast it to a satellite monitoring system where the people following us could retrieve our location.

When the tracker woke up, the spoofer would be broadcasting a counterfeit GPS signal. Being near the tracker, the spoofer would override the signals from the real GPS satellites. The tracker would compute its location using the counterfeit GPS signals and broadcast its bogus position to the monitoring system. To whoever was watching, the tracker would appear to be moving along the route I programmed into the spoofer. I was putting things away and getting ready to take the spoofer up on deck when Mary called out.

"Hey, Finn!"

"Yes?"

"We're about to have company."

Dropping what I was doing, I scrambled into the cockpit. "Where?" I asked, as she handed me the binoculars.

"Back where we came from," she said.

Looking behind us, I saw the white splashes on the northern horizon, even without the binoculars. We were about five miles offshore, and the coast of Puerto Rico made a nice, gray-green backdrop as I watched the speedboat.

"When did you spot them?" I asked.

"Maybe three minutes ago. I couldn't see them without the binoculars then. I watched them until I decided they were headed straight for us. They're coming fast, too."

"Yes. We may have two or three minutes," I said.

I put the binoculars in their holder and opened a small locker in the cockpit coaming. Taking out a folding combat knife, I handed it to her.

"What about for you?"

"I'll use the winch handle. You ready?"

She laughed. "I'm always ready."

"Good. Let's play dumb and see what they do."

"Okay," she said.

I sat down across the cockpit from her, facing aft so I could see the approaching boat. "It's an open boat with two men aboard. Maybe 25 or 30 feet. Two big outboards."

"Sure about that? The two men, I mean?" she asked.

"It's not big enough for anybody to be out of sight."

By then I could see the binoculars hanging from a strap

around the passenger's neck. He leaned toward the man at the steering console and cupped his ear. The man who was steering nodded, and the boat slowed down. They were close enough so we could hear the engines, now. The boat swerved to the starboard and slowed down more.

"Looks like they're coming along the starboard side," I said.

Thirty seconds later, they were alongside, standing off a few yards and matching our speed. I waved, and the passenger waved back, grinning. He bent and opened a big ice chest and took out a fish, holding it up.

"Fresh!" he called. "You wanna buy? Good price."

"No thanks. Just caught a nice tuna."

He dropped the fish and pulled a pistol from his waistband as the boat edged closer to us.

"Heave to or I shoot the bitch," he said, firing a round into the cockpit coaming a foot or two from Mary.

I stood, facing them, and raised my hands as Mary turned our bow into the wind. *Island Girl* coasted to a stop in a couple of boat lengths. As the bow turned through the wind, the jib was backwinded, holding *Island Girl* steady as the swell rolled under us. The man at the wheel of the speed boat reached out and swung three fenders over the side as he brought the boat to a stop.

"Yo, bitch. Stan' up an' raise the hands, like the *maricón* doin'," the man with the pistol yelled.

Mary did as he ordered, and the driver picked up a boathook and pulled them alongside, the fenders screeching as the boats rolled together in the swell. He tied their boat alongside and climbed aboard *Island Girl*, brandishing his own handgun.

"Okay, bitch," the one in the boat said. "You comin' wit' us.

We gon' have some fun. You been missin' a real man, wit' that faggot you hangin' wit'. Come now, or I blow his balls off, if he got any."

Mary climbed down into the speedboat, and the one who was on the side deck came back to the cockpit. Holding his pistol tipped on its side, like the idiots on TV do, he pointed it at me and said, "You gonna live, if you do what we say, *maricón*. Okay?"

"O-okay," I stammered. "Anything. Just don't hurt me."

He grinned and gripped his crotch. "Maybe jus' a little, right at firs', but then you like it, no?"

I did my best to tremble in fear and stammered meaningless syllables as he laughed.

"You jus' wait right there. You don' move, or my frien', he hurt the bitch while you watch. Okay?"

I nodded, shaking, and he put his pistol in his waistband and went below. "Where you got that computer, asshole?" he yelled.

"Lift the lid of the chart table," I said.

I was watching him through the companionway opening, so I didn't see what Mary did. When I sensed movement in the speedboat, I glanced over and saw her easing the inert form of the man to a sitting position. She took his pistol and pushed him sideways, pulling the folding knife from his right kidney. When she looked up and saw me watching, she smiled and blew me a kiss.

The one below deck mounted the companionway ladder, holding on with his right hand as he grasped the laptop in his left. I waited until he set the computer on the bridge deck, not wanting to chance damaging it. Then I swiveled to my right and kicked him square on the chin.

He flew down the companionway backward, landing in a

heap. I was on top of him before he could draw his pistol, but I needn't have worried. Once I got the pistol and stood up, I saw the odd angle his head made with his shoulders.

I turned to go back to the cockpit and saw that Mary was back aboard *Island Girl*.

"Dead?" she asked, peering down at me.

"Yes."

"Damn it, Finn. Why'd you kill him?"

"It was an accident." I shrugged.

"I wanted to question him," she said. "I thought you'd know that."

I eyed the pistol in her hand uneasily. "I didn't mean to kill him. Not my fault he fell wrong."

She saw my eyes following the muzzle of the pistol and put it down on the cockpit seat. "Now what are we going to do?"

"They wouldn't have known anything anyway," I said. "These guys were pickup labor. Help me get him up on deck. We'll put him in their boat and lock the helm. Send 'em on a final boat ride toward Central America."

14

Once we sent our visitors on their way, I said, "I need to finish messing up the tracker, just in case somebody knew those two were trying to grab you."

"All right," Mary said. "But first, let's get underway again. Give me a hand with the sails?"

"Sure."

Mary took the tiller, and I cast off the sheet that held the jib back-winded. As the sail blew across the foredeck, I sheeted it in on the port side, and *Island Girl* accelerated on the starboard tack. Once we were going fast enough for *Island Girl* to answer the helm, Mary said, "Ready about."

"Ready," I said, holding the port jib sheet.

She pushed the tiller over, and I let the port jib sheet run free. Hauling in the starboard one put us back on the port tack, on our original course.

"Good?" I asked.

"Good. I've got us. Go ahead and finish what you were doing."

I took the laptop below and stowed it, picking up the

GPS spoofer. Back on deck, I put on a harness and took the spoofer forward. The most likely hiding place for the tracker was in the life raft's valise, which was lashed to the coachroof in front of the mast. That was the area my scanner pointed to earlier.

Opening the hook and loop closures of the valise, I found the tracker and put the spoofing device right beside it. I pulled the flaps of the valise closed and pressed the hook and loop closures back together.

"Done?" Mary asked, as I joined her in the cockpit.

"Done."

"So you don't think those two were sent to attack us?"

"No, I don't. They were too inept. I think they were local talent. Somebody hired them to put the tracker on board and steal my computer. That's all."

She frowned. "I follow the part about the tracker, but why steal your computer?"

"Nora knows the files are on it."

"They wanted to take me, though. You don't think she sent them?"

"Not to snatch you, no. Nora wouldn't underestimate the two of us; she saw what happened in St. Thomas. If she meant to snatch you, she would have sent the first string into the game, not two bumbling idiots."

"But they knew about the computer, and they were going to take me with them."

"Yes, but I think those clowns were freelancing just now. Whoever Nora sent down here hired them to board the boat while it was unoccupied. Their job was to steal the computer and plant the tracker. They planted the tracker and couldn't find the computer.

"Their lookout probably saw me ashore with the

computer when I was waiting for you. I think they were clueless about who we are. When they saw us leaving, they saw a chance to steal the computer like they were supposed to – and snatch a pretty girl in the bargain. Figured they might as well have a little fun messing with you. Bad boys will be jerks if they get a chance."

"Maybe so. I hope they enjoyed my company enough to make it worth their trouble. But I want to know how they found us to begin with. Or found you. Whichever."

"I've been thinking about that. Maybe I underestimated how desperate Nora is, or how widespread the corruption is."

"I don't understand, Finn."

"I didn't think she'd risk doing the paperwork for a warrant to track my iPhone. The agency would have never done that, back before everything turned to shit. It leaves a trail, and she might have to explain it. And you called me on the iPhone last night."

"But I was using a throwaway phone."

"I didn't mean your call tipped them off. Just that it reminded me I've left the iPhone turned on. Nobody has to call it for them to locate it if they have the proper paperwork."

Mary frowned. "So maybe a crooked judge signed the warrant, you think?"

"Could be. The risk isn't in asking for the warrant. It's in all the people outside their control who get involved in tracking the phone. All it takes is for one person working for a carrier to leak the information, and the secret organization isn't so secret."

"So that's why you think she's desperate? Because she took that risk?"

"Yes. Or there's some other avenue to get the location

information, for the right people in the government. That's why I made the remark about the corruption being more widespread than I first thought."

"What about your iPhone, then? Shouldn't you ditch it?"

"I can set it up as a Wi-Fi-only device and remove the SIM."

"What good is it, then?"

"I can use it with the satellite hotspot for VOIP calls. With a VPN in the loop, it's untraceable, and the communications are heavily encrypted to boot."

"If you say so. Not to change the subject, but I'm starving. I'll fix us some dinner if you'll take the helm."

"Deal," I said.

She went below and started rummaging in the galley.

We didn't eat dinner until almost an hour later, but we both felt smug as we enjoyed the saltfish curry Mary cooked.

"Do you suppose they'll find out about those two morons that came after us?" she asked.

"I don't know. There are too many unknowns for me to even guess."

Mary thought about that for a moment. "Like where the person who hired them is based?"

"That would be part of it. That, and what assets they have at their disposal."

"Assets? You mean people and a boat, right?" she asked. "Those aren't hard to come up with."

"No. But even if they discover those guys are missing, I doubt they'll rush into chasing us without more planning. They've still got the tracker to lead them to us, as far as they know. And if it's my old employer, they don't like operating on U.S. soil.

"That's why they hired two local thugs to do their dirty

work in Puerto Rico. They would prefer to hit us in open water, well outside the territorial limits. And they'll want privacy to interrogate us."

"So you don't think they'll come after us right away?" Mary asked.

"No. They want overwhelming odds of success. That means more coordination. They can't move fast enough to hit us out here without leaving too much to chance."

"They sound like bureaucrats."

"They are."

"How could you work for people like that? Didn't they drive you nuts?"

"I mostly ignored them. I was successful because I didn't play by their rules."

"They let you get away with that? Doing things your own way?"

"As long as they could deny knowing who I was. I was willing to take the risks; others weren't. That's why they kept sending me contract work after I retired."

"They don't have other... um, people like you?"

I shrugged. "I wouldn't know. But if they did, they wouldn't send them in so early in the game. They would wait until they thought we were in a box."

"You think we're safe for a while, then?"

"That's a dangerous assumption. Why do you ask?"

"You could redeem that raincheck, if you think we have a few minutes of privacy."

15

MARY AND I LASHED THE TILLER TO HOLD *ISLAND GIRL* ON course while we got reacquainted. Exhausted, we stretched out on the cockpit seat to catch our breath. After a few minutes, she rolled onto her side, lifting her head from my shoulder and looking at me while she ran a finger along my cheek.

"Can you think of any way besides your phone that they could have found us?" she asked.

"I've been wondering about that. I can't see Nora taking that risk. So I've been retracing my steps."

"Tell me," she said. "I'm curious about what you've been up to, anyway."

I nodded. "When I got back to the BVI from Miami, I cleared out and left for St. Martin that same night. They could have somebody in Her Majesty's Customs on their payroll, I guess. Or maybe they were following the tracker Frankie left on board. But that would only have gotten them as far as St. Martin."

"What did you put on your clearance form when you left there? St. Martin, I mean."

"Fajardo. And remember, I ditched the tracker in St. Martin."

She nodded. "And did you go there? To Fajardo?"

"No. I put it down to lay a false trail. I sailed to Culebra instead."

"How long were you in Culebra?"

"Long enough to clear in. Once I got the message that you were on your way, I left and sailed to Guánica."

"Hmm," she said. "So if they found you in Culebra, that means they discovered you didn't go to Fajardo. They must have found your inbound clearance to Culebra in the U.S. Customs database. How hard would that be?"

"Not too hard, if it was Nora's people. But Aaron would have known if someone did that, most likely. He didn't mention it, and he would have told me if he knew. That kind of work was what he did, so I'm sure he keeps an eye on that stuff now, even though they fired him. They may think they can hide things from him, but they can't. And anyway, by the time they found out I cleared in at Culebra instead of Fajardo, I would have been gone. There's no way they could have known where I was headed. Even if I sailed to another country, I wouldn't have needed any outbound clearance from there."

"They would have had to follow you to Bahia Guánica, then," she said. "Physically follow you. Not likely."

"No, it's not. And nobody but you knew I was going there. I didn't tell a soul."

"You think maybe they followed me?"

"I don't know. Do you?"

She frowned for a few seconds and shook her head. "I

don't see how. Anything's possible, but I didn't make any airline or hotel reservations, even. I didn't want to leave a trail. I just showed up unannounced and took what I could get as far as flights and a room."

"That reminds me," I said. "Who are you these days?"

"Mary Louise Bannon. But I didn't use that identity until I bought my ticket two hours before flight time. And I've never used it before."

We passed a minute or two in silence. Mary broke it with a question.

"Hey, Finn?"

"Yeah?"

"What are the chances somebody else planted the tracker?"

"Somebody else? Besides Nora, or whoever's taking over O'Hanlon's operation?"

"I'm just wondering," she said.

"I guess it's possible, but who? And why?" I asked. "You have any ideas?"

"No, but we should both let that idea rest for a little while. See if anything germinates."

"Okay. You still haven't told me your news."

"No. I'll make us coffee and you get the computer fired up. I've got stuff to show you." She went below and passed the laptop to me through the companionway.

"Do we need internet access?" I asked, thinking of the satellite hotspot.

"No. I've got stuff on a thumb drive."

In a few minutes, we were huddled in front of the laptop, sipping coffee. Mary opened a mind-map file that showed all the connections we knew about between all the players we could name. The only people on her mind-map who weren't part of the O'Hanlon mob were dead, except for Nora and the senator's mystery man.

"Any progress on the mystery man?" I asked.

"Not really. I've got feelers out. I picked up a few vibes, but no firm answers so far."

"I have to ask," I said. "Where is your pal Phorcys in all this?"

Mary sat bolt upright and gave me a harsh look. "Why are you asking?"

"The Florida connection. You said nothing happened there that he didn't — "

"He gave us the senator, Finn. What more do you want?"

"Have you asked him about the mystery man?"

Her eyes flashed. "No, and I'm not about to. It wouldn't be appropriate; he might take offense. Why are you bringing up Phorcys, anyway? And he's not my *pal*."

"Sorry. Didn't mean to strike a nerve." *But it sure looks like I hit one, big-time. What's going on, here?*

"I'm not so sure about that," she said, her eyes like slits.

"About what?"

"Your question. I want to know what's behind it. You're cold and calculating, Finn. Let's be honest with one another, okay?"

"Me? Cold and calculating?"

"Don't you dare try to play innocent. Your 'aw shucks' routine might fool some people, but I know what you are. Out with it; what are you getting at?"

In for a penny, in for a pound, as the Brits say.

"Did you tell him where you were meeting me?"

16

I SAW IT COMING, BUT I COULD TELL FROM THE WAY SHE SWUNG that she wasn't trying to inflict damage. She was just lashing out like a lot of angry women would. I let her slap me, figuring it might lead somewhere worth going.

"You're out of bounds, Finn!"

"It's a reasonable question." I rubbed my cheek. She might not have been trying to inflict real damage, but she packed a hell of a wallop. I wouldn't sit still for another blow like that.

"Reasonable my ass. The only time you've had anything to do with Phorcys, he helped you. Where would your daughter be without him?"

"Try to see it from my point of view, Mary. Yes, I'm grateful that he rescued Abby. I owe him for that. But he didn't do that for me. He did it because you and he — "

This time I caught her wrist before her palm hit my face. I felt her go rigid. Then her arm went limp. I wasn't sure what she was planning, but I felt the subtle shift in her position.

She was about to attack for real, but I took a chance and released my grip. I raised both hands, palms facing her. "Easy. No need for violence. I'm on your side."

Glaring at me, she took a deep breath. I watched as she deliberately relaxed her core muscles. My mind flashed to that tattoo of the cobra on her leg as she struggled to control herself. She was a dangerous woman. *Does she really have that kind of temper, or was that all an act? Not sure I want to find out. At least not right now.*

"You provoked me," she said, after a few seconds. "I shouldn't have let you get under my skin like that."

Maybe that was an apology, maybe not. Probably as close as she's likely to come for now. I nodded, rubbing my cheek again, imagining her handprint on it.

"You have no reason to be jealous of Phorcys."

"I never thought I did. I'm sorry if I gave that impression."

"Then I don't understand why you asked if I told him we were meeting here. You *can't* believe he had this tracker planted on *Island Girl*."

Why wouldn't I think that was a possibility? I kept a neutral expression on my face and let the silence hang.

She was frowning, chewing at a bit of cuticle on her right thumb. I waited. After almost a minute, she took a deep breath and let it out in a sigh.

"What were you about to say?" she asked.

I shook my head and raised my eyebrows. "When?"

"When I slapped you. I'm sorry I lost it, Finn. It's just — my relationship with..." She shook her head. "That's a sensitive area for me. One day, we'll talk about it, but just not yet, please?"

"Fair enough. When you're ready, I'll listen."

"I know. You're the best thing that's happened to me in a

long time, Finn. I don't want to quarrel with you. Now, what were you about to say?"

I nodded, buying myself a few seconds to choose my words. "I wasn't trying to be nosy, Mary. Like you said, you know what I am, what my life's been like. Way back, a mentor of mine taught me to question everything if I wanted to stay alive. He used to say, 'If your mother says she loves you, smile at her. Kiss her on the cheek. But check it out before you turn your back to her.'"

I paused, holding her gaze. Her lips tightened into a line for just a moment, then she forced a smile and nodded.

"Go ahead," she said.

"I meant it when I said I was grateful to Phorcys. I owe him. But what I was about to say is that he did that favor for you; he doesn't know me from Adam. Maybe he would have helped free Abby anyway, just because he's a decent person — I'd like to think so."

I paused for breath, and she nodded.

"But I have no clue whether I can trust him outside my relationship with you. That's not to say I *don't* trust him. I'm willing to, but not on pure faith. I know you *do* trust him, at least within limits. But I don't even know what those limits are. And I'm not pushing you to tell me things that make you uncomfortable. Just trying to explain why I was asking about him. Okay?"

She nodded. "Okay. Thanks for explaining. Sorry again about losing my temper. Where were we?"

17

"THE SENATOR'S MYSTERY MAN," I SAID.

"Right. Now, just so you know, I didn't ask Phorcys about him, okay?"

I nodded, wondering why she didn't.

"That's one of those limits you mentioned, but it has nothing to do with whether I trust him. It's a matter of respecting his privacy. There are some things that I know are off limits with him. I'm on pins and needles when I talk with him; he's scary, sometimes. But he's never turned on me."

"What did you learn about him? The mystery man, I mean. You said you picked up some vibes."

"Nothing the senator didn't tell us, but what I found out confirmed what the senator said. This guy's out there, picking up the pieces of the O'Hanlon mob, or rather his people are. Nobody's seen him. I got reports of other encounters like the senator described — people picked up by two rough guys and blindfolded. Taken to a meeting with the mystery man; being given directions by phone after that.

And the slight accent. Maybe Eastern European, one source said.

"There was this one man who heard about the routine; he got ready in advance. When it came his turn to be picked up for a meeting, he ordered his own muscle to follow along and see where they took him. The guys who picked him up shook the tail, but the blindfolded man didn't know that until later. He had his meeting with the mystery man, thought everything was okay. His body was found a few days later in his office, with every single bone broken."

"Zamochit," I said.

"What?"

"Russians."

"Russians? Zam... what?"

"Zamochit. Back in the days of the Soviet Union, that was the trademark of a Red Mafia hit."

"You think the Russian Mafia's taking over from O'Hanlon?"

"I don't know. Could be that whoever this new guy is, he wants people to think that. Or he really is Russian Mafia. Or he's just a psychopath who thinks that's a cool way to send a signal not to mess with him."

"That's a sick way to kill somebody."

"No argument from me on that. Pure sadism. Any clues as to geography?"

"Geography? You mean — "

"Where have the meetings been? Or I guess I should ask where the *pickups* have been."

"Oh. So far, most of them were in Florida, but there've been a couple in Georgia, and one in Charleston, South Carolina."

"Any pattern you can match to what you know of O'Hanlon's old organization?"

She thought about that for a few seconds and nodded. "There's a good match, but I don't think we've got enough data to draw conclusions yet. Atlanta, Savannah, and Charleston. The ones in Florida were all coastal. But we're talking seaports, except Atlanta, and that's a transportation hub. And a financial center. All key places for the drug business."

"Yeah, or any other business that involves imports, I guess. But," I said, "if you hear hoofbeats, think horses, not zebras."

"Huh? That something else your old mentor said?"

"No. It's another version of Occam's razor — the simplest explanation is the most likely."

"Oh. Okay," Mary said. "You're saying this activity probably isn't a coincidence. I agree. I think whoever this man is, he's taking over from O'Hanlon."

"Where was the man with all his bones broken?"

"Fort Lauderdale. Why?"

"I want to pass that along to Aaron. It's the kind of thing he can work with better than anybody else. Zamochit. That was stupid of our mystery man."

"It made a definite impression on the rest of O'Hanlon's people," Mary said. "Put fear of God into them, for sure. Why do you say it was stupid?"

"It's a trademark; it's unusual. It's not something that your ordinary enforcer would just wake up one morning and think of doing. Or even your ordinary mob boss. Chances are good whoever did it has done it before. It may lead us to him."

"Okay. That makes sense. That's about all the news I have, unless you have more questions."

"I was wondering about the people the mystery man's been meeting with," I said.

"What about them?"

"From what Nora told me a few days ago, and from the things you said then, I got the impression you wiped out most of O'Hanlon's people. Who's left for this new man to meet with?"

"Oh. That's a good question. I took out what you might call the executive tier, the people who reported to O'Hanlon. I figured they were the kind of shitheads who might try to take over, or to set out on their own to build rival operations."

"Right. That's sound logic. So, who's left?"

"Well, I worked my way down a few levels in the organization; the only people left are operational types, worker bees. They don't know much about how all the payoffs and money laundering stuff works. They just move product around and sell it. Or sometimes, people."

"Whoops. You lost me. People?"

"O'Hanlon was dealing in people. Human trafficking was big business for him. Remember, I told you about how they were wholesaling green cards."

"Oh, right, I forgot that."

"And they were exploiting young people — men and women. Forcing them into sex work. The older ones they used to staff sweatshops — laundries, canneries, restaurants — that kind of thing."

"Ugly. You let the people doing that live?"

"For now. I can't kill everybody. I'm focused on cutting off the snake's head."

Which immediately brought to mind her tattoo of the striking cobra, but I suppressed that thought. Neither of us said anything for several seconds. Then Mary broke the silence.

"I'm happy when I'm with you, Finn. Sorry again about earlier."

"Don't worry. We'll have a few more rough spots, I'm sure. But it's worth it. I'm glad you're back."

She leaned over and gave me a kiss on my cheek. It felt much better than her slap. She read my mind, I guess.

"Finn?"

"Yes?"

"I'm really sorry I slapped you. I wish I could take it back."

"Forget it. It's not the first time I've been slapped. But you do pack a good punch. Remind me not to make you really angry."

She snuggled against me and gave me a long kiss. I forgot all about the slap as things escalated.

18

MARY SHOWED ME HOW SORRY SHE WAS. I WAS THINKING IT would be okay if she slapped me more often when she finally excused herself to get a little rest while I took the first watch.

Once she went below, I called out and asked her to dig out my satellite hotspot from the hiding place under the charts in the chart table. She passed it up through the companionway. The laptop was in the cockpit from earlier.

"Thanks."

"You're welcome. You going online?"

"Yes."

"Just making sure it all works? Or are you working on something?"

While I got everything going, I told her about setting up the blind email drop for Aaron earlier in the day.

"Thought I'd see if he's figured out how it works," I said.

"Think he'll have any news on the files?"

"Maybe, but it's probably too early for that. I want to tell him what you learned about the mystery man the senator told us about."

"How much have you shared with him, Finn?"

"Enough so he's got an idea of what's going on. Remember, he worked for Nora; he's been plugged in to this for a while, now."

"Have you told him about me?"

"Not enough that you should worry. He knows you're my lady friend, and that you found the files. But not the specifics, and not your name."

"You sure?"

"I'm sure what I told him. But he's bound to know more. He's probably aware that I asked them to get you that passport a few weeks ago."

"Did you mention that to him?"

"No. And he didn't bring it up. He wouldn't; he keeps his own counsel. You shouldn't worry about him; he would be the first to tell you that he owes me his life. That's an exaggeration, but it's what he believes."

"From your Army days?" she asked.

"Yes."

"How will you explain the questions about Mystery Man?"

"He knows Abby was kidnapped by the people who were after you, and that the files were O'Hanlon's, so I'm not starting from scratch."

"You told me earlier that he knew about Abby from when you were deployed together. But how much?"

"He was my best and only friend when all that happened, Mary. He knows the whole story about my divorce, and Abby. Not the part about me setting up the anonymous college fund, but all the long-ago stuff."

"Finn?"

"Yes?"

"Don't get angry with me for asking this, but could he have accidentally let something about that slip to Nora?"

"No. Idle conversation never happened in our workplace. He never met Nora either. Just like me. They don't even work in the same location; that's all part of maintaining security. I told you, the agency was compartmentalized. Aaron and I worked there for years before we accidentally discovered each other when he gave me that briefing. He and I never maintained casual contact after that. It wasn't done in the agency. They would have probably done away with him — or me — if they discovered we knew one another."

"Why did they let him retire, then? Instead of doing away with him?"

"I told you before, I'm sure they plan to execute both of us. Right now, they're hoping one of us will screw up and lead them to the other. Not to mention that Aaron will be as hard a target as I am. He was the intel specialist on my team, but everybody was trained to kill. Every one of us was deadly, but everybody had a secondary job."

"So why did you end up as a one-trick pony? Or do you have other skills besides killing people?"

"I was cross-trained in all the other member's skills; I could have replaced anybody on the team. At least back then. Some of that stuff's out of date by now."

"What was your secondary job?"

"I was the unit commander. That's why I got all the cross-training. Aaron was my second in command, so he got all the same training I did. My secondary job was dealing with bull-shit from bureaucrats."

"I can't picture you liking that."

"I didn't. And I still don't."

"You said Aaron discovered somebody above Nora greased the skids for her to get your super-secret records."

"Right. And his own."

"So who was it?"

"He thought it was the senator at first."

"You told him about the senator?"

"No. He put that together on his own; asked me if a certain high-profile suicide with ugly secrets was involved in Abby's kidnapping."

"And did you tell him?"

"No. I didn't have to. He knew. That was just his way of letting me know."

"He knew about us killing Senator Lee?"

"No. He's sure to at least suspect *I* did it. He thought Lee was the first one to get those records for Nora; he knows how I would have dealt with that. Lee would have had the authority, but without Nora, he wouldn't have known what to ask for."

"Wait. Back up for a second. He thought Lee was the *first one* to give her the records?"

"Yes. Lee probably set it up for her to get *my* records. Somebody else set her up with access to Aaron's records. Couldn't have been Lee. It just happened yesterday, or the day before at the earliest. So Lee was dead by then."

"Would that have to be Nora's boss? Or the next one up the line?"

"Possibly. Or it's somebody outside the chain of command. Somebody with serious clout. Maybe Mystery Man's got another inside person."

"Sorry, Finn. I've kept you from checking your email drop."

"That's okay. You need to be up to speed on all this, too."
"All right. I'm going to sleep now. See you in four hours."
"Yes ma'am. Sounds good."

19

I FOUND A MESSAGE FROM AARON IN THE DROP.

About that private matter, there's not much information beyond what I already shared. Suspicion, but no way to confirm. It's a dead end for now, but more clues might break something loose. We're working it, but anything you pick up could help, too.

About the encrypted files, there's something strange about them. The name field is encrypted using an AES256 algorithm. That's nearly bulletproof, as far as being able to decrypt it directly. But since they mixed that with the other unencrypted fields, there may be hope. Lots of trial and error, though. It could take a while. We need to find a few names that are pretty certain to be on the list. Then we can back into decrypting the rest.

To come up with names to try, my contacts are using statistical techniques. They're trying to correlate those files that have the encrypted names of recipients of payments with the files containing the bank records. They hope to match the bank transfers with the payment amounts from the file with the encrypted names. Then they think they'll be able to get enough info by hacking the banks' systems to figure out who got the money, at least in a few cases. Those few may be enough to let them crack the coding scheme. If we can get enough data points that way, we should be able to back into that encrypted name field.

Meanwhile, they're trying to figure out why only the payee names got the encryption. Doesn't make sense. Was there a change in command somewhere along the way, maybe? That might explain it, and maybe give us something else we could use. See if your friend knows. I'll keep you posted.

The "private matter" referred to Phorcys; we agreed not to use anything that would identify him, in case Mary happened to look over my shoulder at Aaron's messages. Deleting Aaron's draft, I left him one thanking him for the update. I also told him everything we knew about Mystery Man. Adding what I knew about the Daileys, I mentioned that they kept the files and managed the money for O'Hanlon. But my bet was the Eastern European accent and zamochit would be the critical clues to Mystery Man's identity.

Mary brought a cup of coffee up into the cockpit as I was finishing. Surprised that it was time for her to relieve me, I closed the laptop and turned off the hotspot. Shifting my position to where I could steer with my foot on the tiller, I put an arm around her as she sat down beside me.

"Rest well?" I asked, as she snuggled against me and sipped her coffee.

"Well enough. You sleepy?"

"I think so."

"Did Aaron have anything new?"

"Not much." I gave her a quick rundown on the status of the files. "They're puzzled about why only the payees were encrypted. Why the rest of the files weren't. He wanted me to ask if there was a change in command, as he put it. Like maybe somebody new came on the scene and decided they needed to encrypt the files."

"Or decided they didn't need to, and stopped after they got through the payees," Mary said. "That's a good question, but I don't know the answer."

"I suspected you wouldn't. How long did you know about O'Hanlon?"

She frowned for a few seconds. "I don't understand what you're asking."

"Sorry. Was he somebody you heard of before he hired you to kill the Daileys and recover the files?"

"Oh. No. I heard of the Daileys before. They were high profile people, all over the society pages. Not that I'm a big follower of that kind of thing, but unless you lived under a rock, you couldn't miss hearing about them."

"I'm just trying to understand how you got into all this," I said. "Were they known nationally? Or just in Florida?"

She thought about that as she took another sip of coffee. "Florida, I guess. That's where I spent most of my time, when I wasn't working a target somewhere else. But they probably got national visibility, as prominent as they were in Florida. Why?"

"Like I said, just trying to put things in perspective. So the Daileys were visible and O'Hanlon stayed out of sight?"

She nodded. "Pretty much."

"When you first told me about the Daileys and O'Hanlon, I researched them online. I found the Daileys with no trouble. Even a little about Frankie and his mixed martial arts career. O'Hanlon was a different story. He was tough to find. That matches what you just said."

"What's rolling around in that devious mind, Finn?"

"I'm trying to find a toehold — something to help unravel

all this. You mind telling me how you got the contract to hit the Daileys? I'll understand if you don't want to say."

Mary put her mug down on the seat beside her and gazed off at the western horizon for several seconds. I couldn't tell what was going through her mind. Without turning to look at me, she spoke.

"I'd tell you if I could, but there's not a simple answer." She shook her head, continuing to watch the developing sunset.

After several seconds, just as I was about to break the silence, she continued. "For you, it was simple enough, I guess. Nora or whoever just called you up and told you who you were supposed to kill. It's different for me. I can't exactly have business cards printed up with '1+800-hit-4you' on them, or a web address like 'www.killer-for-hire.com.'"

She still wasn't looking at me. I could see the muscle in her jaw flexing as she clenched her teeth.

"It's done by word of mouth," she said, "but nobody trusts anybody. You can see why. It would be easy to get nailed for conspiracy. So you never hear from the same person twice. There's a network, I guess is the best way to put it."

She turned to face me, but she wouldn't look me in the eye.

After a few seconds, I said, "A network, huh."

She nodded. "It might have been some of the same people; sometimes they used those things that disguise your voice, give it a creepy sound. For a hit, I'd get a series of calls. It was like following a breadcrumb trail or something. No one person ever committed to anything, so if a call was recorded, you couldn't make a case against anybody, even if you knew who they were."

"I don't see how you ever closed a deal that way."

"That's why it works. Once you get through the dance, you end up picking up the info on your target at a blind drop. Sometimes it was physical, sometimes it was a virtual drop."

"How did you avoid getting stiffed on payment?"

"There's an escrow system. The escrow agent thought it was a real estate transaction, as far as I know. They would get word to me that they were holding a certain amount of money to pay me when I delivered the deed. There was an advance, plus there was confirmation from a bank of my choice that the funds were on hand pending my fulfillment of the agreement. Kind of like a letter of credit in international trade. It was double-blind; I didn't know who was paying, and they didn't know who was doing the hit."

"Then how did you and O'Hanlon ever meet?"

"We didn't ever meet. I was taking the files to the drop when his guys jumped me. That's when this whole thing came apart."

"How did you find out he was behind it?"

"One of the guys who jumped me told me when he saw what happened to his partner. Fool. He thought he could make a deal with me, but I had all the leverage."

"They'd already paid you when that happened?"

"Two thirds. I got shafted for $150 grand. I was supposed to get that after I turned over the files."

"O'Hanlon must have known somebody on the inside of the network," I said. "Otherwise, how did his guys know you did the job?"

"He did. He told me before he died."

"He gave you a name?"

She nodded.

"And?"

"And I paid her a visit. She was talkative enough. I started with her, worked my way through several others, but the last one in the line found out I was coming and killed himself."

"How do you know he was the last one?"

"I know, Finn. That's all."

"How many were there in the chain?"

"Does it matter?"

"I guess not," I said. *You're not going to tell me anyway.*

Changing the subject, I asked, "How did you break into the business?"

"Enough, Finn. I'm not ready for any more. Go," she said. "No more of your damned questions."

I leaned forward to kiss her goodnight. She pushed me away.

"See you in four hours," I said, as I went below.

She didn't answer; she wouldn't even look at me.

20

FOUR HOURS LATER, WHEN I CAME ON WATCH AGAIN, MARY was still angry. She gave me the tiller and went below, not saying anything when I told her to sleep well. Earlier in our relationship, I found her hard to read. I didn't have that problem anymore. Or at least not as much.

She was an accomplished liar. She led me the wrong way around Robin Hood's barn as we were getting to know one another, but we were past that. Or so I thought until a few hours ago.

The story she gave me earlier about how she got her assignments made no sense at all. I got a headache just thinking of her made-up tale about the network. She lied again, but why? What was she hiding, at this point?

And she was caught off guard by my questions. She was way too good at lying to fumble the way she did. I just discovered that she didn't improvise well. Before this, I never spotted her lies until long after the fact. I never saw a tell until this evening, but now she was like a rank amateur, looking away, describing a way of doing business that was unworkable, avoiding eye contact. And acting guilty as sin.

I frowned, picking at loose threads. Coming full circle after a few minutes, I shook my head. Why didn't she just refuse to answer? I gave her that option — all but invited her to tell me she wasn't comfortable discussing how she lined up jobs. But instead, she tried to bullshit me. What could that mean?

Then I got a chill when I realized one of the implications of this. She was prepared in advance when she lied to me before. Back then, her stories were coherent and consistent, unlike the bullshit she rattled off a little while ago.

When we first met, I wondered if she had come looking for me. The coincidence of her bumping into me by accident in Puerto Real was unlikely. Somewhere along the way, I suppressed that question. Probably as I was falling in love with her. Remembering my early caution, my reluctance to trust my feelings, I felt like a fool, and not for the first time in our relationship.

The lonely old fart fell prey to a sweet young thing. I even thought at the time that she could be setting a honey trap for me. But she conned me, made me think she felt the same way I did. I felt a hard, black lump forming in my gut.

And a sharp, tearing pain in my chest. Facing up to the idea that she was playing me all this time hurt. After my failed marriage so long ago, I swore I would never fall for another woman. For 20 years, I managed not to do it.

Women came into my life, and women left, but I never let myself feel anything for them. Somehow, I dropped my guard this time and convinced myself that Mary was different. We were soulmates, I thought. But she was playing me the whole time.

That's okay. I've figured it out; from now on, I'm going to play her. She sought me out for a reason. Our first encounter was no accident. She was primed and ready with her series of carefully articulated lies. Each new tale explained away the earlier lies she confessed to, until she finally convinced me she had told me everything. Or at least everything that mattered between us.

The woman was clever; I would give her that. And deadly, too. Don't forget that, you old sucker. Her game's run its course, but she'll never know. Not until I'm ready.

My jaws ached from clenching my teeth. Shaking my head, I dragged myself back to the present. I could do this. I could turn the tables on her, and whoever sent her.

Our interaction would be minimal for the next couple of days. We wouldn't arrive at Isla de Aves until late afternoon the day after tomorrow. This wasn't our first extended voyage together. We usually enjoyed each other's company for a few minutes at watch changes, but I wasn't sure that would happen this time.

She was in a huff when she went below; I would wait and see how she behaved when she came on watch. That would be in about three hours. Between now and then, I would get my mind straight. She most likely would have some tale to try to explain away her anger; I would listen and react in a manner fitting the relationship she thought we had.

There was no point in tipping my hand. If she tried to make amends, I would welcome it with open arms. But I wasn't falling into her trap again. Once bitten, twice shy.

That brought a rueful smile to my face. *Once bitten? You dumb shit. You don't even want to count the bites. But keep the steel in your spine, Finn. That shit stops NOW.*

21

Forty-four hours later, *Island Girl* swung to her anchor in the relatively calm water in the lee of Isla de Aves. Mary was off watch, asleep on the settee in the main saloon.

Tucked in behind the lee cloth we rigged so we wouldn't fall off the settee in rough water, she was oblivious to our arrival. I let her sleep.

Our trip from Bahia de Guánica was rough. The weather was squally for the whole two days. We made good time under reduced sail, but the trip wasn't conducive to reconciliation.

Neither of us rested well during our off watches, and Mary was angry to begin with. Lack of sleep didn't improve her mood. She continued to give every sign that she was still as upset as she was right after our set-to at the beginning of the trip.

That suited me all right; I was happy enough to use the time to lick my wounds and get my head straight. I wasn't over my hurt and anger, but I was in control of my feelings at this point. That was all that mattered.

Sitting in the cockpit, I watched the black clouds and lightning bolts out to the west. That was the most recent squall, the one that hammered us two hours earlier. The forecast I picked up before I came on watch said the low-pressure area would be well away from us by morning. From the looks of the sky, the worst was already over.

Bending at the waist as I sat in the cockpit, I could see the barometer on the bulkhead just beyond where Mary slept. The pressure was rising steadily for the last few hours. We were in for a quiet night and a pretty day in the morning.

Careful not to wake Mary, I slipped below and dug two cold beers out of the icebox. I took them back up to the cockpit and settled down to watch the sunset. Filtered through the last of the storm clouds, it would either be spectacular or a non-event, depending on how far the last squall moved in the next hour.

Retrieving my bag of snacks from the cockpit's footwell, I found a salami and provolone sandwich to go with my beer. I popped the first can and took a sip, savoring it after 48 hours of drinking only water or tepid coffee.

Pulling the plastic wrap from the sandwich, I took a bite and chewed slowly, propping my feet on the opposite seat and leaning back. Sailing definitely offered its own rewards. People who never spent 48 hours without sleep while being battered by storms at sea couldn't imagine how wonderful a salami sandwich and a beer could taste. Enjoying them while watching a tropical sunset from a calm anchorage made them even better.

As I filled my belly, I wondered what the next few days would hold for my relationship with Mary. We were here because she wanted to experience having an island to ourselves. Maybe her mood would improve. I hoped so.

Even though my trust in her was shaken, maybe even broken, she could be good company. And with the storms out of the way, this was about as romantic a spot as she could want. Maybe we would enjoy ourselves; I resolved to do my best, anyhow. And I hoped she would, whatever she was up to.

Since my exchange with Aaron the first night out, neither of us had been in touch with anyone ashore since we left Puerto Rico. We could have used the satellite hotspot to check email, but neither of us did. Turning on the SSB marine radio every few hours for an updated weather forecast was as close as we got to contact with civilization.

One thing that pleased both of us was that the lousy weather stretched all the way north into the Bahamas. If whoever planted that tracker was up there trying to intercept us, they weren't having a good trip either.

Thinking of the tracker made me wonder again how those people found us in Bahia de Guánica. Given my renewed suspicion about Mary, I thought it was likely that she led them to us somehow. I couldn't fathom why she would do that. She wasn't careless, but it seemed the only explanation.

Maybe Mary was grouchy because I screwed up her play, whatever it was. Or maybe her anger was unrelated to the questions I asked.

For a moment, I considered dragging the laptop and the hotspot up here. I could check the email drop Aaron and I were using. After two days, he might have news, either of the decryption of the files or of Mystery Man. Or both. He wouldn't say anything else about Phorcys unless I gave him the all clear, at this point.

I spent a lot of my on-watch time over the last two days

wondering about Phorcys. Phorcys and Medusa. Mary and
Phorcys. Did she get her jobs through him? Was that what
she was trying to cover up with her bullshit story?

If so, why did that matter, between the two of us? There
was something off about her relationship with Phorcys; that
was clear. She mentioned that dealing with him made her
anxious — on pins and needles, was the way she described
her reaction to talking with him.

Mary wasn't a woman who was easily frightened. She let
me listen in on her last two calls to him, back when we were
working to rescue my daughter from her kidnappers. From
what I heard, he was favorably disposed toward Mary; he
even said he owed her favors.

The way he sounded, he owed her more than he was ever
likely to be able to repay. So why did he make her nervous?
Or was she just feeding me more bullshit to hide something
else about their relationship?

Before I finished with Mary, I would know. Or one of us
would die because of my trying to find out.

I finished my sandwich and washed it down with a
swallow of beer. The sunset was shaping up nicely. There
were enough storm clouds on the horizon to diffuse the light
and turn the sky to a palette of colors ranging from yellow to
orange to scarlet to deep red.

Opening my second beer, I slugged it down as I watched
the show. I finished the beer as the sky faded to gray and
black. It was time for me to creep into the forward cabin and
get a full night's sleep.

22

ONE OF THE BEST PARTS OF HAVING MARY ABOARD WAS WAKING up to the smell of fresh-brewed coffee. I lay in the V-berth, taking my time getting up, thinking about how that coffee was going to taste.

I was feeling good about life in general. Then I remembered Mary and I were on the outs. At least I was well-rested. And she made coffee. Maybe she would share it. I crawled out of the V-berth and put on a clean pair of cutoffs and a fresh T-shirt.

It was early. The gray light filtering into the cabin was just enough for me to see what I was doing. I made my way up into the cockpit where I found Mary nursing a mug of coffee and waiting for the sunrise.

"Morning," she said, pouring coffee from the thermos into another mug and holding it out toward me.

"Thanks," I said, taking the coffee and holding it under my nose, inhaling the aroma before I took my first sip. "Good morning yourself. Been up long?"

"Long enough to make coffee. I tried to be quiet and let you sleep. Sorry if I woke you."

"Thanks. You didn't wake me; I went to sleep right at sunset. Must have slept 12 hours. You rest well?"

"I did. I was whipped. I didn't even hear you drop the anchor last night. When I woke up, it took me a few minutes to figure out why we weren't bashing into the waves anymore. This is a fine spot, and it looks like we're going to have a clear day."

"That's the last forecast I heard. The low's moved off toward Central America. Supposed to be nice, settled weather for the next several days, at least."

She was sitting at the aft end of the port side of the cockpit, facing forward, looking east. I sat at the forward end of the starboard side, looking diagonally across the cockpit at her. In the dim light, I watched her face fall when I didn't sit beside her. Looking down at her feet, she took a sip of coffee.

After a few seconds of silence, she said, "Finn?"

"Mm?"

"I'm sorry I've been such a bitch for the last two days. I have problems, but I was wrong to take them out on you. Forgive me?"

"Sure," I said. "I thought I pissed you off asking too many questions."

"No. No, you didn't. I... Well, maybe that spurred me on, I guess. You did make me angry, but... frustrated, more. And plain old scared. I shouldn't have felt that way. I know I can trust you, but this is new to me."

"New," I nodded. I took a sip of coffee before I said, "Me, too. I think I know what you mean."

She studied me in silence for several seconds, her face expressionless. Then she shook her head. "Thanks for trying to understand, but there's just no way you can. Understand, I mean. I've spent the last two days trying to figure this all out, and I'm still not there. There's just so much shit I..."

I let the silence hang while I took several swallows of coffee. "Want to tell me?"

She looked me in the eye for a second, squinting and chewing on her lower lip. "Yes. But I don't know how yet. I owe you the truth, this time. I know I must have about run out of rope with you, and that's the scariest feeling I've ever had. I don't want to screw this up. Not this time. But I'm so ashamed..."

I nodded, giving her time.

"I've told so many lies that I'm having trouble remembering the truth. I don't mean just to you — to myself, too. I've heard drug addicts describe losing their grip on reality. I can only guess at what they mean, but that's how I feel."

I didn't say anything.

"I don't mean now. Now I feel like I'm waking up, kind of. Seeing things the way they really are after living in some kind of hazy hell for as long as I can remember. And how things really are is awful. But I don't..." She shook her head. "I'm so afraid."

I saw tears begin to trickle down her cheeks.

"We're about to get a spectacular sunrise, and we're in a beautiful spot — our own little desert island," I said. "There's nobody to bother us. Nobody even knows where we are. This is a good spot for getting reacquainted with yourself. I'm not going to ask you any more questions — no pressure. If you get to a point where you want to talk, I'm here. If you don't, that's okay, too. And if you need out, we'll sail to wherever you want, and we can part ways. No pressure. All right?"

She nodded, sniffling, rubbing her nose with the back of

her hand. "Thanks, Finn. Maybe you do understand. I don't deserve you."

"Maybe you deserve me, maybe not. I'm no angel. You don't know enough about me to make that call right now. One step at a time. How about if you sit here and enjoy the sunrise while I go fry up a few flying fish and eggs? Maybe some grits?"

"Okay," she sobbed, watching me get up and go down the companionway ladder.

As I gathered the stuff for breakfast, I heard her start bawling uncontrollably.

My instinct was to go back to her and take her in my arms, but I resisted. I wanted to comfort her, but I needed to keep my distance and let her work through this.

If she did come clean somehow, it would have to be without my help. I didn't know what she was dealing with. This might be more of her bullshit, for all I knew. But I didn't think so. *That might be the voice of hope, trying to triumph over experience. Keep your distance, Finn. It's okay to feel sympathy for her, but don't let it cloud your judgment.*

As hard as it would be, I would just have to wait until she revealed the next version of her tale, if that's what this was. Or for her to come to terms with whatever was bothering her, if she really was working toward some sort of reconciliation. I fought enough of my own demons to know that beating them requires a solitary effort.

23

AFTER BREAKFAST, MARY TOOK THE DINGHY AND WENT ASHORE to explore Isla de Aves. She didn't say she wanted to be alone, but she didn't invite me, either. She needed time to herself; I would let her have as much as she wanted.

I watched as she beached the dinghy and tied it off to a piece of broken concrete well above the high-water mark. She set off across the narrow strip of sandy ground, disturbing the terns that were nesting everywhere. They fluttered into the air, screeching at her, and then settled down as soon as she was a few feet beyond them.

She carried an insulated lunch bag. Tucked under her arm was a rolled-up beach blanket.

We were anchored about 50 yards from shore, and the island itself was less than 100 yards wide. There was just enough high ground between us so that when she reached the beach on the windward side and spread her blanket, she was out of my line of sight.

After she was settled, I powered up my satellite hotspot and started to check the email drop I was sharing with

Aaron. Before I got the web browser open, I saw the notification flag on my regular email client's icon; there were two emails waiting.

I used that email client to access a plain old email account. It was independent of the accounts I used for secure communication with Aaron and Mary. It was for more normal things — banking, travel reservations, keeping up with casual contacts — that kind of stuff. And for last-ditch, coded messages from Nora, when all else failed.

I wasn't expecting any regular email. The two messages were probably spam, but I decided to look at them anyway. Mary was planning to stay ashore for most of the day; I wasn't pressed for time.

The emails were from two pharmacies in India. They each offered a drug to cure my erectile dysfunction. The logos of the two drug companies were almost identical.

To anyone else, the messages would look like spam. To me, each logo was a signal that I should call a pre-established emergency contact number. Nora wanted to talk with me, and she knew the satellite phone wasn't working.

I took a more careful look at the messages. There was a subtle difference hidden in the text embedded in the two logos. The messages were from different people.

The emergency contact number would be answered by an automated system that would prompt me to enter a four-digit code. There was a default code, which I memorized long ago along with the emergency number. That code was for me to use when I initiated the contact procedure. These messages gave me two different four-digit codes, the equivalent of different extensions.

One message was sure to be from Nora, but what about the other one? There was no reason she would have sent two messages — no reason I could think of, anyhow. One message was sent yesterday; the other was time-stamped from the day before.

Odds were that the first one was from Nora. The second one intrigued me. Who could have sent it? Why? Was Nora being shut out? Or had someone tried to reach me before Nora could?

The only way to get answers would be to call both numbers. I could guess what Nora would have to say, so I was more interested in the second message. I would respond first to the message less likely to be from Nora.

There was no cellphone service out here, but I could use Wi-Fi calling from my iPhone via the satellite hotspot. That offered the advantage of being far more secure than a cellular call.

Wi-Fi calls, or VOIP calls, as they were more correctly known, were difficult to trace. They were impossible to tap. The data packets of encoded audio were protected by end-to-end encryption, and sequential packets didn't follow the same physical path between the two endpoints.

Before I called either number, I checked the email drop to see what was new with Aaron. Our last contact was two days ago; he could have learned a lot since then. Sure enough, there were two messages from him in the drafts folder.

I opened the one with the older date first.

I have an update on those files. They include checking account statements from seven different banks. The transactions were spread among the different banks to get around the Bank Secrecy Act's reporting requirements. Whoever is running this is no amateur.

My source matched bank transactions with the "payoffs" file.

This is taking longer than we expected. There's trial and error involved to find which payments add up to a specific payoff amount.

We thought we could identify one of the recipients from bank records of the receiving banks. We hacked into the receiving banks' systems to find the account holder. That was a test to see if our approach worked.

We didn't manage to identify the account holder before we were subjected to a cyberattack that wiped out our entire online system. Clearly, we hit a virtual tripwire, so we know our theory is correct. We kept offline backups, so we didn't lose any data, but we're working to identify the source of the cyberattack.

Until we figure out what happened, we've suspended further work on the decryption. Once we find the tripwire and figure out how to avoid it, we'll try again. For what it's worth, my source has never encountered anything like this before; this level of security is unprecedented. I thought you should know what you're up against.

About the mystery man, we're still pulling in bits and pieces, but suspect Russian government involvement. Possible that there may be more than one mystery man. Several suspected FSB / former KGB agents have shown up in the areas you flagged at around the right times.

We're being careful on this. We've learned there is a super-secret Department of Justice investigation touching on our candidates for the mystery man. The same DOJ investigation is looking into the recent murder of an FBI agent in St. Thomas. Can't confirm yet, but suspect it may be the man you mentioned.

I'll update as I have new info.

I reread that several times, committing it to memory before I erased it. Then I opened his second message.

When you're alone and have time to talk, call me at the last number we used.

After I erased that one, I left him an acknowledgement. He might not be available to take my call in the next few minutes, so I wanted him to know I understood his messages.

Before I made any phone calls, I stood up, trying for enough height to see over the rise in the island. Mary probably wouldn't come back while I was on the phone, but I wanted to make sure of that.

Unable to see across the low dunes, I went forward and climbed up the mast a few feet. Mary was stretched out on her blanket, sunbathing. Since I was downwind from her, she wouldn't be able to overhear my phone calls.

Back in the cockpit, I connected my iPhone to the hotspot's Wi-Fi and dialed Aaron's most recent number.

24

"YEAH?" AARON'S VOICE WAS GRUFF, PITCHED LOWER THAN normal, like he was disguising it.

His phone probably showed "Caller ID not available" for the incoming call.

"I'm trying to reach Elena Howard. I got a message to call her at this number. She there, by any chance?" That was enough for him to recognize my voice.

"You get my messages?"

"Yeah, that's why I'm calling."

"Okay, but what's with the caller ID block?"

"It's a VOIP call, through a VPN and a satellite hotspot."

"Okay, that's cool. You by yourself?"

"For the moment. She's ashore right now. I'll be able to see her coming before she can tell what I'm up to. What's up?"

"Phorcys. We think it's the name of an organization. Maybe also the guy who runs it, but not his real name. Their objectives are consistent with what I told you before. We got a little finer definition, but it doesn't add much of consequence. Not as far as we know yet, anyhow."

"What's that mean?" I asked.

"I told you how my source felt about them, right?"

"You said she thought they could do no wrong."

"That's maybe a bit of an overstatement. They're willing to cross some lines, but nothing you or I would worry about. Their goal is to keep the government in the hands of strict constitutionalists."

"You mean conservatives?"

"Well, definitions are tough. Let's say they favor the middle two-thirds of the ideological range. Not too far to the right or to the left."

"So what lines have they crossed?"

"Rumor has it they've taken out a few rogue politicians, but they're selective as all hell about it."

"Proven crooks?"

"There are signs that they've set up some of those — boxed them in with solid proof and made sure the authorities took them down. Same thing with the wing-nuts."

"Wing-nuts are one thing, but what about the crooked ones? What happens when the authorities won't act? Say somebody's on the take?"

"I'll get to that soon. First, listen to their party line, okay?"

"Okay. Tell me."

"Their stated mission is to compel elected officials to uphold their sworn oaths to preserve, protect, and defend the constitution. Some people think Phorcys was started by a few retired senior military officers. Word is they were fed up with the way our government was behaving. Their goal's supposedly to function as a watchdog — they watch the watchers."

"They sound like an upstanding bunch, to me. But they're anonymous?"

"That's right. Maybe they are upstanding; I don't know. It's hard to fault their party line, but there are other rumors you should know about."

"Okay."

"They have a small branch called something like 'Special Projects,' or maybe the 'Projects Executive.'"

"'Special projects?' 'Projects executive?' Any idea what that means in plain English?"

"'SPG,' we've heard they call it. Also 'PE,' but we aren't sure those are the same thing. This gets to your question about real live crooked politicians. When there's criminal activity and the government turns a blind eye, Phorcys refers the problem to SPG, and the traitors end up dead."

"How sure are your people about this?"

"Not sure at all. But you asked. Remember that suicide we talked about after Abby was rescued?"

"Yes," I said, feeling goosebumps along my spine. "What about it?"

"That was investigated by the best team the feds could pull together. Somebody way up the line didn't buy that he killed himself."

"In your message you mentioned a secret Department of Justice investigation into the crooked FBI agent's death."

"Yeah, and into some of the candidates for Mystery Man, too. That's one investigation. This one was separate from that."

"Did they find anything?"

"Not directly related to the cause of his death, no. But did you hear that a bunch of incriminating shit came out about him right afterward?"

"I've been out of touch. What kind of incriminating shit?"

"He was apparently a sick bastard — into stuff so kinky it would curl your damn hair just to think about. Rumor was that he knew it was all about to hit the media, and that's why he killed himself."

"So?" I remembered Mary and Phorcys referring to something like this, but I kept that to myself.

"So there was a problem with the incriminating material. He had a mistress, which was no big secret."

"Okay. I'm not following. What about the mistress?"

"She was in the Bahamas when he supposedly killed himself. She told the cops he was due to meet her there the day his body was found. With me so far?"

"Yeah. So the cops found her?"

"She found them. Called homicide in Miami after she heard the news about him. Flew back at their request and spent several days interviewing with them. Seems that he had an alibi for the times when he was supposed to have done some of that kinky shit."

"The mistress? Was she the alibi?"

"The mistress and two other people, yeah."

"So where's this going?" I asked.

"Nowhere. The mistress and the other witnesses are missing."

"Missing?"

"Yeah. There was evidence of foul play in the mistress's case, but it led nowhere. Case closed. The other two are just plain gone. No trace to show they ever even existed. They weren't exactly paragons of virtue, I guess. Not like anybody would get too upset about their disappearance. Anyhow, the team the feds put on it backed the finding that it was a suicide and shut down the follow-up investigation. Somebody with stroke decided it was best to let it be, if you want my guess."

"Okay. Does anybody think Phorcys was behind any of this? Either the senator's death or the disappearance of the alibi witnesses?"

"I don't know. You think Phorcys played a part in it?"

"Sounds like that's a dangerous thing to contemplate," I said.

"Yeah, I agree. You want me to keep after this?"

"No, let it go. But if you happen to hear anything else, pass it on to me, okay?"

"You got it. I may have more on the files in the next day or two. But my source on that DOJ investigation's trying to reach me on another line. She thought she was onto something hot. Check the blind drop this evening, in case she gets something."

"Will do."

"Gotta take her call; anything else that's hot while we're on the line?"

"No, nothing. Thanks; I'll be in touch after I get the next package from you." I disconnected the call and sat back to think about what Aaron told me, and what he didn't tell me.

He knew I would read between the lines. Aaron would never ask, but I could tell he thought I was behind that suicide. And he would be pretty sure Mary was involved in it, too. His comments on the mistress and the other witnesses were interesting.

Mary's time wasn't accounted for during the period when the mistress and the witnesses vanished. As far as I knew, she was in Florida then. My bet was that she took care of cleaning up those details while I was sailing back and forth to St. Martin. But I wouldn't ask. People in our line of work didn't ask each other questions like that; it was considered rude.

Before I responded to Nora and whoever the other person was, I needed coffee. I went below and put the pot on the stove, planning my calls while it perked.

25

BACK IN THE COCKPIT WITH A THERMOS OF COFFEE, I POURED myself a mug and picked up my phone. My first call was to the person I suspected was *not* Nora. After I keyed in the four-digit code from the email, I heard a man's voice repeat the four digits.

"Speak," he ordered, after he rattled off the numbers.

"There's no fun in erectile dysfunction. I hope the shit you're selling works. If it doesn't, I'm gonna saddle up and come kick the — "

"All right," he said. "That's enough. Your voice is authenticated. Your caller ID's not showing up. You on a secure line?"

"Yes. I'm using VOIP through a satellite connection to a VPN."

"Okay. Good enough. I'm going to run through the details of your missions in order, starting back in 2001 and working toward the recent hit in Antigua. When you're satisfied that I'm legit, stop me. Questions?"

"Maybe. Let's see how you do first."

"Fine," he said. "In February, 2001..."

He recited a history of my jobs with enough detail to surprise me. He gave me more information than what I originally reported on two of them, causing me to wonder who was watching me back then. After the fifth one, I stopped him.

"Satisfied?" he asked.

"For now. What do I call you?"

"Boss will do. The woman you used to take orders from for the last 20 years? She still reports to me. Take your time and carefully parse what I just said. Then tell me how you interpret it." He paused.

Okay, so this is Nora's boss — an undersecretary in the Department of Defense, whose name's a closely guarded secret. I replayed his statement in my head. He said, "Boss will do." Then "... you *used to take orders...*" and "... she *still reports...*" The disconnect in tense was significant. He was telling me I no longer reported to Nora, but she continued to report to him.

"You're implying that I now report directly to you," I said.

"Good so far. Keep going."

"She still works for you; she's still there."

"Close enough. You're a good listener. She's reporting to me, but she's been working for somebody on the outside on the sly for a while now. She doesn't know I found her out. You following me?"

"Yes. So far, but where is this going?"

"First, I have a question. I know she sent you a message a couple of days ago. Basically like the one from me you just responded to, but with her callback code." He gave me the four-digit callback code from Nora's message, and then said, "I know you haven't responded directly to that message; I'm monitoring her calls."

"That's correct," I said.

"Have you been in touch with her through an alternative means since you got rid of the sat phone she gave you in St. Martin?"

He knows something about my meeting with her in St. Martin. And that I ditched the sat phone. Does he know where I was when I last used it?

"No. How much do you know about what happened in St. Thomas?" I asked.

"We'll get there. Just bear with me. I'm feeling my way with you. Do you understand?"

He's not sure where my loyalty lies. Neither am I, but it certainly doesn't lie with Nora. Play along; see where he goes with this. Maybe I can trust him, maybe not.

"Sure. I understand."

"Are we okay on time? Can you spare several more minutes? Or do you need to call me back later?"

"I have plenty of time."

"Good. I'll play a recording for you. You'll recognize one voice. The other doesn't matter for the moment. I want your reaction, so listen carefully. You ready?"

"Ready," I said.

"Here goes."

I heard a click, followed by a few seconds of the hissing of a poor-quality recording. Then I heard Nora's voice over the hiss.

"I need your help with a little project," she said.

"Happy to help, Phyllis. What do you need?" I recognized Senator Jefferson Davis Lee's baritone southern drawl with no trouble.

"I've told you not to use names, damn it."

"Sorry. Don't sweat it, though. This line's swept every day. It's clean."

"With all due respect, you don't know shit about that kind of thing. Watch what you say. I've told you before; you should always assume someone's listening."

"Okay, sorry. You're right; I'm not used to this spook stuff. What do you need?" Lee asked.

"There's a girl at the University in Gainesville. Her name's Abigail Carroll." Nora spelled the last name. "Her address is 1701 Southwest 16th Street, Apartment 201. You got that?"

"Yes. Got it. What about her? Want me to get her an internship or something?"

"No. I want you to have someone kidnap her and hold her for leverage. She's the daughter of that guy who's helping the woman we're looking for. The one who has those files we want."

"That woman's the one who killed — "

"Shut up, dumbass." She cut him off. "No names."

"Right. Sorry again. So, you want me to have someone pick up the girl?"

"Yes. Make sure it can't come back to you; the guy and the woman are dangerous. You understand?"

"Yes, sure. Dangerous." He coughed. "What happens once we have the girl?"

"Okay, pay close attention. They're not to harm the girl without my explicit orders. They should take a photo of her and send a text to the following number with the picture and the message I'm about to dictate. You ready to write it down?"

"Yes."

She gave him the number of my iPhone and began to

dictate. *"She's a pretty girl. Don't worry. We won't do anything to spoil her looks. Wouldn't want to reduce her market value. In case our friend in St. Thomas forgot to tell you before he died, we want the girl who was calling herself Mary Elizabeth O'Brien. And we want to know who has copies of the files she stole from the Daileys. You have 48 hours to deliver. After that, we'll send you videos every six hours showing what we're doing to this sweet child until you give us what we want. Keep your phone close by."*

"That's it? You want their names in there? You said — "

"I know what I said. Yes, I want the names in there. Have them send that text to him word for word. Make sure they use a burner phone and ditch it right away. He may come after them."

"Okay. I got it."

"Any questions?"

"Yes. What happens to the girl after we get the files and the woman?"

"You can give the girl to the people who snatch her, for all I care. In fact, that would be best. They need to make sure she doesn't surface afterward. Maybe send her on a long, long trip." Nora laughed.

Lee chuckled. "She pretty?"

"I have no idea. What difference does that make?"

"The people I'll use have a market for — "

"Shut up, you dumb bastard. I told you I don't care what happens to her afterward. That's up to you and your people. But make sure they don't touch her until I say different. This guy's no amateur. He'll want to talk to her, probably want a video call with her. Understand?"

"Yes. And is that allowed?"

"Yes. We want him hooked solidly. He has to know she's okay, but that's it. If he thinks they're abusing her, there's no telling what he might do. She needs to be unharmed so she can talk with him, but no drawn-out conversations. If he doesn't follow instructions, then we'll mess her up and make a video of it, but nothing too permanent. We don't want to lessen his incentive to cooperate, okay?"

"I got it. When do you want this done?"

"Yesterday. Don't screw it up, or you'll pay dearly."

"Yes, ma'am."

There was a click, and my new boss came on the line again. "You get all that?"

"Yes." *I decided to test him a little.* "Who was the man she was talking with?"

"Look, I'm not sure how your dealings with your former boss worked, but you're playing in a different league now. Don't ask irrelevant questions. Clear?"

"Yes, sir."

"Good. Just so you don't wonder, I know who Abigail Carroll is, and what she means to you. Okay?"

"Yes."

"That never happened, what they were talking about. That's all been handled. There's no further threat to Abigail, and they never touched her. Don't worry about it. I played the recording to let you know what your former boss was trying to do to you and yours. You pissed off at her?"

"Yes." *What does he think happened with Abby? He recorded Nora's conversation with Lee. Does he not know they went through with the kidnapping?*

"Good. Just FYI, the person she was talking to killed himself before they snatched the girl. Hold onto that anger for a while, though."

Okay, he's got the timing screwed up, somehow. Thinks the senator killed himself before he went through with the kidnap-

ping. So he doesn't know it wasn't a suicide. I'm disappointed in these people. I've invested 20 years with them. Now I find out Nora's a crook, and her boss is a dimwit.

"What you were going to ask about St. Thomas — did it have to do with your boss supposedly getting killed in your presence?" he asked.

"Yes."

"I thought so. I know about that. The other business, the Abigail thing, they were planning to use that for extra leverage, but we took care of it without your boss knowing exactly what happened."

Nice try, asshole. You just blew your credibility, for sure. "I see. That's a relief."

"We're looking out for you. It's the least we can do, in view of your service to the country. Back to St. Thomas — afterward, she was planning to go to you and feed you a story about trying to set up the man who supposedly killed her. Did she get to you with that story?"

"Yes."

"How did she reach you?"

"We were using a pair of off-the-books encrypted satellite phones." *You mentioned that earlier in this conversation.*

"Right. I just wanted to be sure. We've got her phone under surveillance, but we think you destroyed the mate, the one she gave you in St. Martin after you took care of the ISIS bastard. That right? Did you ditch it in the Miami airport?"

He's trying to show that they know all about me. Fool.

"No. Right after she called me, some locals in the BVI stole it." *Might as well confuse things for them.* "I confess that I left it on the table in a bar where it would be easy pickings for the local druggies. Practically begged 'em to steal it. I figured she was working for the wrong side when I got the call from her after what happened in St. Thomas. I didn't want her to track me through that phone. You say it was found in Miami?"

"She told me her people tracked it to the airport there. Found it in the trash, minus the SIM and the battery. You weren't in Miami?"

"No. Be interesting to know who had it and how it got there."

She told me in St. Martin that tracking wasn't enabled on that phone, but I didn't believe her. I was right.

"Yeah. She couldn't figure out what you were doing in Miami. Stolen, huh? That explains it."

"Guess whoever stole it sold it or traded it to somebody for dope," I said. "Stolen sat phones are in demand on the black market down here. Smugglers buy them, figuring it's that much harder to track than a cell phone. Wonder why they pulled the SIM? They usually just use them until whoever lost it gets the service turned off." *Never mind that a thief wouldn't have been able to get past the lock screen on that phone.*

"No idea. Okay. I'm feeling better about you; glad we got to talk through this. You ready to take it to the next level?"

"Maybe. What's the next level?" I asked.

"I like you; I like your track record. Your old boss, she's got to go. You understand?"

"Yes."

"I thought you would. But I have two problems. Interested in helping me out?"

"What are the problems?"

"The first one is that we need to debrief her — fully. I need everything she knows. Names, places, motivations —

everything about the people she betrayed us to. You know the drill, right?"

"Yes. And after she's been wrung dry?"

"She's of no further use. In fact, she'll be a huge liability. You know what that means."

"Sure."

"You willing to take that on? The whole thing, from interrogation to termination?"

"It's what I do. Why not?"

"Good. Any questions before we get into the mission briefing?"

"You mentioned two problems. She's one; what's the other?"

He chuckled. "She's actually both problems. After she's gone, I need somebody to take her place. You interested?"

"I'm interested. But let's deal with one problem at a time, if it's okay with you."

"Sure. Here's my idea, but I'm open to your suggestions. You're the pro at operations. I think you should call her in response to that email and let her lead you. I want you to give me until tomorrow before you call her. Okay so far?"

"Yes. I'll call her tomorrow. Then what?"

"She's put out the word that you've gone rogue. Surprised?"

"No. Not after what happened with the setup in St. Thomas. I didn't buy her bullshit."

"Of course not. Based on her saying you've gone rogue, I will give her a warrant for your execution. Because of your sensitive background, I'm ordering her to supervise your interrogation and termination. She'll have an assassin with her; you're a hard target, and she knows it better than anybody. But the assassin will have orders directly from me to turn your old boss over to you and leave you alone, unless you ask for help from her."

"Ask for help from her, who?"

"The assassin will be a woman. What do you think?"

"Sounds good to me. I think that's all I need. Unless you say otherwise, I'll call my old boss in the morning and set this in motion."

"Good. Let me know if you need anything, but call me in the morning before you call her, just to make sure I've set her up. Let's continue to use this contact scheme for now."

"Okay."

"Pleasure talking with you. Look forward to working with you." He disconnected the call.

My coffee was cold. I dumped it over the side and refilled the mug from the thermos. There was still no sign that Mary would return soon, which suited me. There were loose threads in the story Nora's boss tried to weave. I wanted to pick through them while our conversation was fresh in my mind.

SIPPING MY FRESH MUG OF COFFEE, I SORTED THROUGH ALL THE information from Nora's boss. Over the years, I developed my own mental filing techniques. In my college days, I found that doodling on a letter-sized pad was a good way to organize my thoughts. Once I finished drawing circles and arrows and scribbling comments about what they meant, I didn't need to refer to my notes again.

My work required solid memory skills, but writing notes was dangerous. Nevertheless, I knew that writing things out helped embed facts in my memory. Early in my work, I weaned myself from using paper notes.

I learned to close my eyes and visualize a yellow legal pad. With an imaginary fountain pen — don't ask me why; it works, so I stick to it — I doodle to my heart's content. When I finish mapping out whatever problem I'm struggling with, I open my eyes and my notes vanish. But the information doesn't. It's all nicely catalogued in my mind; ready for recall any time I need it.

The strangest part is what happens when I recall it. In

my mind's eye, I see everything I need, all organized and written out neatly on the pages of a yellow legal pad.

That's not how I visualize the information when I'm processing it into my memory. It's jumbled and illegible, then. But when I call it up, the notes are presented in flawless script. The mind is a marvelous puzzle.

I dealt with the phone call to Nora's boss first. Aaron's information would keep. Besides, Aaron presented it in a logically connected fashion, which made it easier to remember. Nora's boss — I'm going to think of him as just plain "The Boss," from now on.

The information I gleaned from my phone call with the boss was a mess. His delivery was disorganized, maybe by design, and when I tried to put the pieces together, there were inconsistencies.

Inconsistencies are part of the real world. Things rarely fit together without gaps and conflicts, and when they do, it sets off warning bells. Fabricated stories don't have conflicts; the truth is a ragged piece of work, full of holes and contradictions.

On a macro level, I didn't trust the boss. I put that at the top of my first imaginary yellow page. *The boss is full of shit.* I went on from there, listing my thoughts and recollections as they popped into my mind, brainstorming as opposed to trying to impose order.

He was definitely who he said he was. He knew too many insignificant details to be an impostor. All that stuff about my early missions — he was reading from the files. After he mentioned things, I remembered them. But it was stuff I did, and even I couldn't have called up that kind of detail off the top of my head. So he read the files, or excerpts from the files.

Nora told him about meeting me in St. Martin. He knew she

gave me the satellite phone when we were there. Then later he asked about the phone like he wondered where I got it and pretended he did that on purpose. Why? Did he forget? Was he a clumsy liar, or was he trying to trip me up somehow?

He claimed he caught Nora working for "somebody on the outside." But he didn't say who, or how long she'd been under suspicion. Or how he caught her. Nora was a consummate professional. She wouldn't have left an easy trail to follow.

And she would never have let that call with the senator get recorded. That was an amateur's error. So she probably recorded it herself. Maybe for leverage over the senator.

But then how did the boss get the recording? Did she give it to him? Why would she do that?

The boss acted like he thought I never got the text about Abby. Did he really think the kidnapping was planned but not executed? He said as much.

The text with Abby's picture was supposed to go to my phone. How would he think I didn't know? Unless he really believes the senator killed himself before it was sent, before the kidnapping took place.

And the text Nora dictated was a verbatim match for the one I got. That nails Nora without a doubt. Not that I questioned her guilt, but that really ices it.

The kidnapping, the rescue, and the "suicide" — all that happened in a short period. If the boss wasn't in on it before it happened, Nora could have told him the senator freaked out and overdosed. Maybe because he couldn't cope with the demands Nora made on him, or something like that.

But that means Nora was briefing the boss on this whole plan, doesn't it? Or is there some way the boss could be an innocent dupe? If he had the recording, though, she couldn't have fooled him, could she?

Maybe she could have. She might have spun him a yarn about trying to set the senator up. Then she could have given the boss the recording. She might have claimed the senator's suicide proved his guilt.

Does he really believe the senator committed suicide? He didn't give any sign that he thought otherwise. But he also said something like, "That's all been handled. Nothing's going to happen to Abigail." He was implying that the agency had something to do with preventing her from being kidnapped. But that didn't make sense, either, if Nora set up the whole thing.

I knew Abby was kidnapped. And the senator ordered it and knew it happened. He told me so himself when Mary and I questioned him. Further, he confessed that Nora, or "Phyllis," as he called her, had told him about Abby.

But in another universe, maybe Abby didn't get kidnapped, because the senator died before he gave the order. He could have killed himself, or been killed. That didn't matter. In that universe, I could see Nora giving the recording to the boss to justify executing the senator.

That would mean Nora played her boss. That could have happened. She could have even made him think the senator was killed on his orders, after she played the recording for him.

In that alternate universe, then the boss might be an innocent victim of the conniving woman I once worked for.

That made a nice story, but it conflicted with the boss's own story about catching Nora working for somebody on the outside. If he caught her out, he wouldn't have believed what she told him about the senator.

So where does that leave you, Finn?

Where it left me was confused. But that was okay. I wrote everything down on my imaginary legal pad.

When I went back to it later, it would make more sense.

That's how my memory trick worked. After making sure there was nothing more to add, I opened my eyes and the legal pad vanished into the recesses of my mind.

When I raised the coffee mug to my lips, I found it was empty. I opened the thermos and poured myself another shot of coffee. Taking a swallow, I shifted my thoughts to my conversation with Aaron. I didn't need to use my memory tricks this time.

27

WHAT AARON TOLD ME ABOUT THE CYBERATTACK SHOWED THE scope of the criminal conspiracy that Mary and I were up against. The mob using virtual tripwires to protect their bank accounts took me by surprise.

Thinking about that for a few seconds, I realized it was no more surprising than their penetration of the agency. Few people, even high-level people in the government, knew of our existence. *Ouch. Not sure I want to use "our" regarding the agency anymore. Not after that recent conversation. That's not the operation I signed up to work for — not now, anyhow. Maybe it used to be, but "used to be" doesn't cut it. Gotta get used to thinking of the agency and the mob as the same. Scary thought, but deal with your reaction later, Finn.*

And then there was the mystery man, with potential ties to the Russian Mafia. That was just another name for Russia's government, these days. Was the mystery man pulling O'Hanlon's strings before Mary blew O'Hanlon away? Good chance, now that I thought about it.

The intricacy of the tripwire and the cyberattack argued that this conspiracy developed gradually. It wasn't put together overnight to seize the opportunity afforded by O'Hanlon's demise.

Mary might have some insight into that notion. I was disappointed that I couldn't kick it around with her. But right now, I wasn't sure where Mary and I stood. And that thought led me to Aaron's comments on Phorcys.

His information made me less comfortable about my relationship with Mary. Though I resisted it, I kept coming to the conclusion that Mary could be part of Phorcys if it were an organization.

I considered Phorcys might have just hired her for a hit on somebody. But when she let me listen in on that conversation with her contact there about freeing Abby, he implied that he was deeply in her debt.

That meant their relationship went beyond just a contract killing or two. Mary's price for the Dailey hit was $450,000, from what she told me. Unless she was lying, O'Hanlon — not Phorcys — hired her for that job.

Assuming she charged Phorcys that kind of money, I couldn't imagine how they would feel indebted to her. Unless whatever she did for them was more involved than her normal service, I couldn't account for the depth of their gratitude.

At her request, they tracked down the kidnappers and their bosses. "Contract intelligence operatives. Not your garden variety thugs at all," Phorcys had called them. Plus, they interrogated and dispatched them and set up the senator for us. That went way beyond a casual favor, and Phorcys told her he still owed her. I was missing something.

Weighing against that worrisome situation was Aaron's description of the goals of Phorcys. As he described them, they weren't bad people; they were committed to the same things I was.

He referred to "their stated mission." His choice of words puzzled me. It almost sounded like he was reading from a brochure, or a website. Given the shadowy nature of such organizations, that wasn't likely.

He was tapping a source; maybe someone inside Phorcys. It was tough to know where Aaron got his information. Given our relationship, if I asked, he would tell me, but I wouldn't put him in that position.

I could, however, lean on him to see how much credence he gave the source. Making a mental note to press him on that, I moved on to think about his other intelligence on Phorcys.

There was a part of their organization called "Special Projects Guidance, or SPG." Or, he said, "maybe the 'projects executive.'" From what he said, SPG/PE dealt with enforcement. He made it sound like an in-house special operations team that handled dirty work, up to and including assassination. With access to resources like that, why would Phorcys call on Mary?

Aaron even mentioned the smear job that was carried out to lend credibility to the senator's "suicide." That reminded me again of the phone call with Phorcys that Mary let me listen to. Back then, I thought she was talking to a *man* called Phorcys. Now, I wasn't sure. But his identity didn't matter as much as what he said. I couldn't recall his exact words, but he referred to the smear material, and then offered to take care of the senator for her.

Mary declined his offer. She told him dealing with the senator was a personal matter. She was right; it definitely was personal. But that exchange confirmed what Aaron said about Phorcys referring "the problem to SPG, and the traitors end up dead."

The other piece of information I took away from Aaron's references to the senator was that Phorcys fumbled the smear campaign. Whether that was evidence of sloppy work on their part or just plain bad luck, it meant they were forced to clean up after themselves. And the cleaning up involved making three witnesses disappear.

I wondered again if that's how Mary spent her three days in Florida. If so, was she paid by Phorcys? Or was that another favor she did for them? A favor like that would put them even further in her debt.

Aaron also mentioned that someone high in the government stopped the investigation into the senator's death. From the context, Aaron thought it was someone who was part of the O'Hanlon/Russian Mafia conspiracy. I wondered if it could be someone working for Phorcys instead. We would probably never know. And I wasn't sure it mattered.

I had a more immediate problem. What was going to happen between me and Mary?

Sitting in the cockpit facing aft, I noticed the sun was getting low in the sky. I missed lunch, not that it mattered. But Mary would be back soon.

Maybe I'm psychic, or maybe the breeze carried a sound that triggered my thought of Mary. Either way, seconds after the thought, I heard the outboard sputter to life 50 yards off *Island Girl's* bow. Mary was coming.

Before I could get my feet under me, I felt the gentle

nudge of the inflatable against *Island Girl's* side. The outboard went silent as I turned to look over my shoulder.

"Hey, sailor," Mary said, as she clambered over the life-lines and bent to tie off the dinghy. "Buy a girl a drink? We need to talk."

28

"RUM PUNCH?" I ASKED, GETTING TO MY FEET.

Mary settled herself in the cockpit. She shook her head, a somber look on her face.

"Maybe later. For now, I need a clear head. Orange juice for me, but help yourself to some punch."

I went below and poured two glasses of cold orange juice. Back up in the cockpit, I handed her one and sat down on the bench seat across the footwell from her. I waited, watching as she took a sip of juice. Swallowing and licking her lips, she looked me in the eye. She took a deep breath and sighed.

"There's no way to do this except to just do it," she said.

I nodded, waiting.

"I've told you before, you're the best thing that ever happened to me, Finn. I know you think I'm just a kid, but I've lived hard and fast. I haven't been a kid since my early teens. I've known a lot of men along the way, but you're the first one I've ever fallen in love with. I'm not sure I like it, this being in love stuff. But I can't shake it. I've tried."

She paused and took a sip of juice. I held her eye and kept my mouth shut, giving her another little nod.

"I've wanted to tell you the truth, but I was scared. Not much scares me, at this stage of my life. Just about every bad thing you can imagine has already happened to me, and I've survived. But losing you terrifies me. I've been trying to come to grips with that; I couldn't admit it to myself at first, but there it is."

She paused. Taking another deep breath, she held my gaze for several seconds. Nodding, careful to keep a neutral expression on my face, I would let her say what she needed to say without my giving her any cues.

"I've been a shitty person, Finn. Sorry there's not a more refined way to put it, but there's not. Shitty is the best adjective to describe my behavior. I'm not talking about the hand I was dealt. No excuses. I'm talking about how I played it."

She paused, squinting a little as she looked into my eyes. "I need to hear your voice, please. Say something, anything?"

I looked back at her, trying to think of what to say. Her anxiety was palpable. "I know this must be hard for you. But I can tell it's important to you. Keep going."

She nodded. "Thanks, Finn. Plenty of people have bad childhoods. Maybe worse than mine, some of them. I don't know. But that's not an excuse. I *liked* a lot of the shitty things I had to do to get by. I pretended to myself that I didn't have choices, and at first, maybe I didn't. But later on, I did, and I kept doing shitty things because I enjoyed them. I never stopped to think about what I was becoming until I met you. But now I'm ashamed of the things I did, a lot of them. Not the killing; you know about that. I told you I never killed anybody that wouldn't have done the same to me if the tables were turned. I know you understand that. You following me?"

"I think so, yes."

"I don't know if you can, really. I won't put you through a graphic description of the life I led before I met you. Not that I'm trying to hide all that; it happened. If you need to hear me talk about what it was like to — "

"No, Mary," I said. "This is about what you need, not what I need. Tell me what you need for me to know."

She took another sip of her juice and nodded, looking into the distance and swallowing with difficulty. Tears rolled down her cheeks. She blinked and wiped them away with the back of her hand, looking me in the eye again.

"Someday I may need to tell you all that stuff — the stuff I did when I was... before I..." She stopped and shook her head. "The part that troubles me most... That's what I need to tell you. And that all has to do with you, with us, really. Okay?"

"Yes." I waited. *What's with all the tears? This woman's a cold-blooded killer.*

She sniffled for a few seconds and said, "It wasn't an accident that I met you in Puerto Real."

I was stunned. I suspected as much, early on. But somehow, I suppressed my suspicion to the point of forgetting it. Once I collected myself, I saw that she was watching me. She cried quietly, waiting.

"I'm so sorry to do that to you, Finn. But that's the worst part. At least for me it is."

29

THIS TIME, IT WAS MY TURN TO SWALLOW HARD AND TAKE A deep breath. I sighed and caught Mary's eye again. "Okay. I'm all right, just disappointed. Tell me whatever else you need to tell me."

"I know you have questions. I'd rather you let me talk, but if you have to stop me and ask questions, that's okay. I've spent the day trying to figure out how to tell you this without tangling it up with my own emotions. The lie I've been living since that day on the dinghy dock is the worst thing I've ever done. I've tried to anticipate your questions by putting myself in your position. Tell me how you want me to do this."

"Just go ahead. I'm too dazed to come up with coherent questions at this point. Better if you take the lead, I think. But take it in small steps, okay?"

"Okay, but stop me if you need to ask something. All right?"

"Yes."

"Phorcys sent me. They knew about your mission to kill Dimitrovsky in St. Vincent. They wanted him dead, too. You were ordered to kill him, but they said Nora fed you misinformation. It was O'Hanlon who wanted him killed, not the government. At least that's what I was told. Maybe the government... that doesn't matter. O'Hanlon was pissed because Dimitrovsky was bypassing him, somehow, working with someone who was trying to cut O'Hanlon out. O'Hanlon knew about your mission; he and Nora were using you to settle an internal squabble in the mob. The three people who attacked me in Bequia were looking for you. They were sent by Frankie Dailey, but they missed you and got me. Frankie was double-crossing O'Hanlon, working for whoever Dimitrovsky was in cahoots with. But O'Hanlon didn't know that. With me so far?"

"Yes."

"The three men in Puerto Real," she said. "I think they were after you, too — not me. That's the only thing that makes sense to me. Frankie probably sent them, and when they struck out, he sent the team that hit us in Bequia. I know you have questions; I see it on your face."

"Yes. I'm trying to take all this in, but there's a big disconnect already. When we got to Ste. Anne, they — "

"Snatched me off the street," she interrupted. "Right? That's your disconnect?"

"Yes."

"They wanted you. They planned to use me for bait."

"So they knew you had the files all along, then?"

"They knew a woman had the files, but they didn't know I was the woman. They thought I was just some girl you picked up. Not until you copied the files onto that microSD card and gave it to Nora. Then they knew, but that was later."

"But O'Hanlon hired you to kill the Daileys and retrieve the files."

"I won't blame you if you never trust me again, Finn. But I have to come clean with you. Whatever happens between us is just going to have to happen."

"I don't understand."

"I know. The other big lie I told was that O'Hanlon hired me. He didn't. I was working for Phorcys all along."

But Frankie told me you were a hired killer working for O'Hanlon.

"But wait. You're saying Phorcys hired you to kill the Daileys, then?"

"Phorcys hired me to get the files from the Daileys. Killing them was an option, but the plan was for me to copy the files without the Daileys knowing. I really did work for them for a little while, sort of. Not long enough to find out where the files were, though. The Daileys... well, let's just say they invited me to their house one night for... reasons I'd rather not talk about. I told you, I've done things I'm — "

"Okay," I said, holding up my hand, palm toward her. "Never mind why they invited you there. What happened?"

"I was in their bedroom, waiting for them to join me, when I heard this commotion out in the main living area. Frankie burst in on them. I heard Mrs. Dailey call him by name, and then there were gunshots, and screams from the Daileys.

"He kneecapped them right at the start. His own parents. Then he demanded to know where the files were. They tried not to tell him, but he tortured both of them, taking turns. I don't know what he did to them, but it went on for a long time, the screaming did. Then his mother told him about the safe, and the combination.

"I overheard that. The safe was in their bedroom; I cleaned it out and left through a door that opened onto a patio before Frankie came into the bedroom. While he was occupied with them, I got away. Sick bastard. And they told me he left them alive while he went to get the files, in case they lied to him."

"They told you?"

"I wasn't lying about his muscle catching up with me. They told me all about it, all the gory details. They thought they were going to have their way with me, and they started out by telling me all that, thinking it would soften me up."

"But how did Frankie and O'Hanlon know you took the files?"

"When Frankie went into their bedroom and found the safe open, he went back to work on his parents. He said they told him I was in their room, and that I must have taken the files."

"He said? When did you talk with him?"

"Right after his thugs caught me. He told them to take me to his place in Atlanta and start working on me. He had something else to do in Florida before he could join in the fun, as he put it."

"And you escaped."

"Yes. Before he got to Atlanta. That part of my tale was true. But they didn't know who I really was. Not at that point. I was disguised. They thought I was just a high-priced escort the Daileys found somewhere."

"But they snatched you in Ste. Anne. They must have known who you were by then. You said they didn't know until I gave Nora copies of the files."

She shook her head. "They thought I was just some girl you picked up, like I said. Nobody there recognized me."

"Frankie told me that O'Hanlon hired you — the girl they snatched in Ste. Anne — to kill the Daileys and steal the files. He said you were supposed to give them to O'Hanlon, but you took off."

"He told you that? In Ste. Anne?"

"Yes."

"I know what you're thinking, Finn. I don't blame you; I've told you so many lies..."

"But?" I asked.

"But I'm telling you the truth, at least as I know it. I don't know how Frankie made that connection. He was the only one who would have recognized me as the escort, and he never saw me in Ste. Anne. He was waiting for you on *Island Girl* when they caught me. That's what O'Hanlon told me right before I got the drop on him. All along, I thought they didn't know I was the escort who stole the files. The people in Bequia didn't mention the files to me. They wanted you, to stop you from getting to Dimitrovsky. How could..." She shook her head.

"You told me about the files, that they were chasing you because of them."

She clenched her jaw for a second or two and locked eyes with me. "Just one more lie on my part. I couldn't tell you the truth at that point, that I was hired by Phorcys to protect you and make sure you could carry out your mission. It was sort of true, the story about the files. By then, I wanted to tell you everything, but I thought I was in too deep."

She stopped talking and just looked at me. I stared back at her. The silence hung between us like a thick, black fog. And then it hit me. She might be telling the truth. Or what she thought was the truth.

"What was the escort's name?" I asked.

"What? I don't — "

"The name you were using when you were with the

Daileys, when Frankie's men captured you and took you to Atlanta. What was it?"

"I don't remember what I told the Daileys, but the only identity I had when they caught me was Mary Elizabeth O'Brien. The one I was using when I met you. It was safe, as far as I knew. Why?"

"Any way they could have known about it? Picked up on it somehow?"

"The two guys who were holding me went through my purse before I escaped. I see where you're going with this, but I killed them, Finn."

"You told me at one point that they drugged you."

"That's true. When we were driving to Atlanta. They... you think maybe they told Frankie? Before I killed them?"

"Could they have?"

"Maybe. You think..." She was frowning, shaking her head.

"Frankie told me they had a source in customs and immigration in St. Vincent," I said. "That's how his people found us there. If you're right, they were looking for me. But they might have picked up Mary Elizabeth O'Brien's trail by accident."

"I never thought of that. The three people in Bequia might not have known, but there was time for Frankie to put all that together before we got to Ste. Anne. He would have known I was on the boat with you. Even though we changed our identities before we got to Ste. Anne, they put that tracker on the boat in Bequia."

"Yes, and then there's that identity I got for you before we went to Ste. Anne."

"Right. Mary Helen Maloney. What about it?"

"Nora knew about it. And she would have known about

the O'Brien one, too. All at once, because they used the O'Brien passport reference to get into the State Department's passport files. That's how they generated the Maloney passport for you."

"You're right, Finn. So they did know who I was by the time we got to Ste. Anne. What else can I tell you? Now I've lost track of all the things I thought I should fill you in about."

"They'll come back to you, if they're important. Meanwhile, tell me about Phorcys," I said.

"I told you about Phorcys hiring me. What else do you want to know about them?"

"Looking after me isn't the first job you've done for them."

"No, it isn't. They're a... well, for lack of a better term, a regular customer."

"A regular customer?"

"Yes." She frowned. "What are you asking?"

"Not your employer?"

"No. I'm in business for myself. You're asking that because of what my contact said about favors?"

"Partly. Who is he?"

"I don't know. He's been my regular contact there, but we've never met. Kind of like you and Nora, I guess."

"How did you come to take jobs with them?"

"I work through an agent, a broker. She's part of a network, of sorts. She takes a commission on the jobs she sets me up with. And she provides a cutout for both parties, usually. Phorcys became an exception, because they use me often. They book me through the broker, but they brief me directly."

"What else do you know about them? Phorcys, I mean?"

"Nothing I can think of. Why?"

"You said they hired you to copy the Dailey's files."

"That's right."

"And did you deliver them?"

"Eventually, yes."

"Eventually?"

"I told you about O'Hanlon's people ambushing me when I was on my way to the drop?"

"Yes. Is that true? It really happened?"

"Yes. That messed up the original handoff. Phorcys was alarmed, worried that there was a leak somewhere that allowed O'Hanlon to set that up. They were busy sorting that out, so I didn't get them a copy of the files until right before I left Florida to fly to San Juan."

"Do they know they don't have the only copy?"

"Yes. They're okay with that."

"Do they know I'm working with someone to get the files decrypted?"

"Yes. That's not a problem to them. Is it a problem to your contact?"

"I don't know yet. Maybe, but that's a topic for later."

"Later?" she said. "I'm afraid to ask, but I can't stand it, Finn. Do we have a later?"

"I think so. I'm not sure what it's going to be like, but nothing you've told me changes how I feel."

"Even after all my deception?"

"We both live in that kind of world, Mary."

"But how can you possibly trust me?"

"I don't trust you. Not yet. Maybe not for a long time. But I still love you. That's not the same as believing everything you tell me. I trust your feelings, not your words. Can you cope with that?"

She nodded, blinking back tears. "Thank you, Finn. That's more than I hoped for. I love you."

"And I love you," I said. "I'm no better at this romance business than you are."

"You have more questions?" she asked, sniffling.

"I will, I'm sure. And so will you. Plus, I have stuff to tell you, to talk over with you. I need your opinion on several things. And your help. But none of that's important right now."

"It's not?"

"No."

"What's important?"

"Come here. I'll show you while we watch the sunset."

She did, and I did.

30

MARY AND I ENJOYED A NICE DINNER IN THE COCKPIT AFTER
sundown. We were lingering over the last of the wine when
she said, "We needed this; I needed this. Thanks, Finn. I
haven't felt so at peace since I met you."

"I'm glad. Glad we met, whatever set it in motion. And
glad you feel at peace."

"I do. This is a magical spot, you know?"

"What makes it magical to you?" I asked.

"We could be the only people in the world. It feels like
we're anchored out in the middle of the ocean. We're all
alone, in this tiny spot where the seas are calm, with a strong
trade wind blowing and the waves breaking on the reefs.
And it's a beautiful evening."

I couldn't think of anything to add to that. She was snuggled against me with my arm over her shoulders, so I just
gave her a squeeze.

"I don't want to spoil it," she said, "but you said earlier
you had things you wanted to talk about. Should we do
that?"

"I suppose. Even in a magical place, life intrudes."

"What's on your mind?" she asked, sitting up and taking a sip of her wine.

I told her about my conversation with Nora's boss. She listened without interrupting, and when I finished, she didn't say anything for a long time — maybe 30 seconds, but to me, it seemed like an eternity. I raised my wineglass and took a full swallow.

"I can't make sense of that," she said. "I get that he wants you to get rid of Nora and take her place. But unless you left out something, he doesn't have the straight story on what happened with Abby and the senator."

"I didn't leave out anything."

"Then how can you explain his misunderstanding?"

"I can't. Not very well. What bothers *you* most about that?"

"For him to think you'd buy his story, he would have to believe you didn't know about Abby's kidnapping. That's just nuts."

"Yes. Or?"

She looked up at me, her brow furrowed. After a few seconds, she said, "Or he thinks it didn't happen. Do you think he believes the senator killed himself rather than carrying out Nora's plan?"

Interesting that she thought of that. I was careful not to suggest the idea to her. I stuck to reciting what he said.

"He would have to, unless he's part of it."

"Part of it?"

"Part of Nora's scheme."

"Which do you believe?" Mary asked.

"I don't want to bias you with my conclusions; I don't trust my objectivity, here. Ask me anything else you want to and I'll answer, but not about my opinions. Not yet. I need your fresh ideas."

"Okay, fair enough. You're sure about that recording?"

"I'm not clear on what you're asking. What about the recording?"

"Are you sure it was Nora and Senator Lee?"

"Yes."

"You said Lee told her his phones were checked for bugs daily. Is that right?"

"Yes. Why?"

"I'm trying to understand how her boss got that recording. Do you believe Lee about his phones?"

"No reason not to. He had plenty of reason to worry. We know that."

She nodded. "So that means the tap was most likely on Nora's end. But she was the one warning him. Besides, that seems unlikely given her background. From everything you've told me about her, she's extra cautious about that kind of thing. Right?"

"Yes."

"After 20 years of experience," Mary said, "she somehow let her phone call get recorded? I don't believe that."

Good! Neither do I. Now, where are you going with that?

"Then how did her boss get that recording?" I asked.

"Nora knew about it, Finn. She had to know her boss was recording that call. Or she recorded it herself. She would have been way more circumspect, anyway. About what she said, I mean, naming me, naming the Daileys. Don't you think? Unless she wanted all that information in the recording."

"Yes. So what do you think happened, there?" I asked.

"They were setting up the senator, maybe?"

"Maybe," I said.

She took a drink of her wine and said nothing for a few seconds. "Or," she said, "they made the recording for some other reason — some reason we don't know about — but they decided they wanted you to hear it at this point."

"But why? Phorcys freed Abby, and we killed the senator. They may not know the details about Phorcys, and we were careful not to leave any evidence that contradicted the notion of suicide. But they're guaranteed to suspect I had a hand in all that. Probably suspect you, too. I mean, Nora even warned the senator about us on the recording."

Should I tell her about Aaron's comments on the investigation into the senator's death? Maybe, but not yet. That might lead into the whole Phorcys thing. I'm going to come clean with her on that soon. It's only fair. But I don't want to distract her right now. She's on a roll.

Mary shook her head. "You're supposed to call her in the morning?"

"Yes. The boss asked me to wait a day, so he could set her up."

"Did he give any sign he might know about the tracker we have on board?"

"No. What makes you ask about that now?"

"A day's delay. Maybe he was buying time for something besides setting her up."

"Like what?" I asked.

"I don't know. Ambushing us, maybe. I'm thinking out loud. You said he knew you didn't respond to her message?"

"That's right. He said he was monitoring her calls."

"If she were hiding stuff from him, she would expect that, wouldn't she? Expect that he might monitor her calls, I mean."

"Yes, probably so."

"Are there other ways she could communicate with you? I mean, if she assumed her normal channels were compromised. You must have had more than one fallback method in case the special satellite phones didn't work."

"Yes. But that one with the hidden four-digit code embedded in a logo in a spam email is preferred."

"Why?"

"It's secure and it's fast. The other ways don't offer such a quick turnaround."

"Have you checked them? The other ways?"

"Well, yes. They don't require me to do anything in particular. I'd get an email, to that same account."

"Then you'd have to check your email, even if they used one of the other fallbacks? Do they all depend on email? The same email account for you?"

"There are several, but the fallbacks aren't dependent on email. I don't have to check my email; it's just one way I would know they were trying to reach me. I'll give you an example. I have a checking account set up for online banking. They can send me a signal by making a deposit followed by a withdrawal. The amounts and the interval between them are predetermined, but the source and destination of the funds could be anything. That all happens electronically. The account is set up to send me an email notification when there's an authorized third-party withdrawal. But if I think my email account is compromised and I don't want to check it, I can check the bank account online, or even by phone. You follow?"

"Yes. But that assumes you have a reason to check. You say the others are similar?"

"That's right. But normally, if the sat phones weren't

working, I would be on the lookout for a contact. That would be a reason for me to check without depending on email. I wouldn't wait for an email. The others involve credit card accounts, online subscriptions, that sort of thing. They work about the same way the bank account does."

"Okay. So how do you respond, once you know they're trying to reach you?"

"There are a variety of blind drop arrangements. Eventually it comes down to a roundabout telephone call with someone whose voice I would recognize, or who has the right challenge and response phrases."

"I see. But you didn't get any of those email notifications?"

"No. Why?"

"It seems strange that both Nora and her boss used the same means to get in touch with you, especially if one of them doesn't trust the other."

"You're right. I didn't put that together."

"What do you suppose would have happened if you called Nora first?"

I thought about that for a few seconds. I wrestled with which number to use before I made the call that ended up being to the boss. But it didn't occur to me to consider what Mary just asked. "She would have told me her boss was crooked, probably, and given me a kill order for him," I said, after pondering the question. "Like a mirror image of what he told me."

"Uh-huh. That's my bet, too. And that can only mean one thing, Finn. You agree?"

"I need to hear you say it, please. To be sure I'm not drinking my own bath water."

"Yuck! That's a vile image."

"Sorry. Back to the point you were making?"

"They're working together. It's a setup; they're after you, Finn. How's that sound?"

"No different coming from you. It's what I think, too."

"You wanted to take Nora out, anyway; they just made it a little easier to justify, right?"

"Maybe. But now we can't stop with Nora. We know her boss is part of this."

"So we go after him, too," Mary said.

"That's the idea, but he's a tougher target, since I don't know who he is. And Nora's going to come to us. He'll be too careful to do that."

"I'll bet we can make Nora tell us," Mary said.

"I'm pretty sure she doesn't know. But it might be satisfying to try."

"Do you have any other ideas to discover his identity?"

"Yes. Some. Do you?"

"Phorcys owes me, big time. And you're thinking you can put your friend Aaron on it, I'll bet."

I nodded. "Between the two, one of them might find out. Or at least come up with some leads. Speaking of Aaron and Phorcys, that's something else I need to discuss with you."

"I wondered when that was coming. I know people are asking about Phorcys. You're behind that, aren't you?"

"Have we been sloppy? Or is Phorcys that good?"

She laughed. That rich, mesmerizing laugh I loved to hear — and I had not heard it for too long. "Neither. It's what I would have done, if I were in your position. That's all. I would have been disappointed in you otherwise. So, can you share what you learned?"

"Yes, but it's probably nothing you don't know."

"Oh, don't be too sure. I've told you what I know about

Phorcys, which isn't much. I may be more curious about them than you are. But there's something we should do before we start that."

"What's that?"

"I'm salty and sandy from sitting on that windward beach all day. I need a shower. Join me? Then we can crawl into the V-berth and you can tell me all about Phorcys. I've missed you, Finn. I've felt distant from you even when I was with you, because I've been — "

"I understand," I said, standing up and taking her hand to lead her below.

31

AFTER WE WERE BOTH SHOWERED, WE CLEANED UP THE GALLEY from our dinner preparations and I filled Mary in on what I learned from Aaron while she was ashore. I gave it to her in order, beginning with the files.

"I'm having trouble with this, Finn," she said, after hearing of the cyberattack. "That's way over my head. A cyberattack? I've heard the phrase, but what is that, even?"

"Where are you losing track?"

She shook her head. "When they hacked into the bank system. I can at least follow along with the concepts until then. But this tripwire idea is new to me. How does that work?"

"I'm not up on the details, but it's probably akin to being locked out of your online banking if you enter the wrong password too many times. I'm sure it's more complicated, but — "

"Okay, but they weren't locked out. How could the attackers wipe out their whole system?"

"You're in denial, Mary. Quit trying to convince yourself it didn't happen. It did. Aaron has no reason to make that up."

She was frowning, unable to let go of her skepticism.

"Let's say that instead of locking them out, the bank's system pretended to let them in and sent them a virus or something; some file that got through their firewall and then morphed into an executable that locked up their system. That stuff's way over my head, too, except Aaron said it happened. And maybe the malware didn't come from the bank. Maybe trying to hack into the bank triggered it to come from somewhere else. I don't know how that stuff works."

"Okay. Then that means they're stuck for now, as far as the files," she said. "Right?"

"Right. You said Phorcys has the files, now. They'll try to decrypt them, won't they?"

"I'm sure they will. I didn't discuss that with them. My deal was to deliver the files, so as far as they're concerned, I'm done."

"Do you think you might be able to find out anything from your contact? Without causing a blowup?"

"Maybe. Let me think about how to ask; I have to give some logical reason why I need the information. Otherwise, it would set off alarms. You said your friend found some info on Phorcys?"

"Yes. We'll get there, but let me take it in order, so I don't forget anything."

"Sure," Mary said. "Go ahead."

"The next thing was the mystery man. They were still piecing stuff together, but they think it's a Russian operation. They — "

"Russian operation?" she asked. "You mean the Russian Mafia's behind the mystery man?"

"They think it's the Russian government — not sure there's much difference. But they think there may be more than one person, too. Aaron said they've found several possible agents in the places you pointed to. So, it may not be one person."

"Was that Dimitrovsky man you killed in St. Vincent a Russian? The name sounds Russian."

"We didn't know about his national origin for sure. He was a Russian agent, wherever he was from. He was feeding money to extremists in the States, stirring up any kind of trouble he could. You said Phorcys sent you to make sure I got him. Any idea why they cared?"

"No. But maybe I can find out. If I'm going to call in favors and start asking questions, I might as well get 'em all on the table. But you wanted to talk about the mystery man. Are we ready to move on to Phorcys?"

"Not quite. Some of the people Aaron said were candidates for our mystery man are the targets of an ultra-hush-hush DOJ investigation."

"Really? How did he find out, if it's so hush-hush?"

"He doesn't tell me things like that, unless there's a reason. But that's not all. The same DOJ investigation is looking into the killing of an FBI agent in St. Thomas."

"Kelley?" she asked.

"That's Aaron's guess, but he's trying to get confirmation."

"What could that mean, Finn? I'm feeling a little overwhelmed, here."

"You and me both. I can't even guess, except there must be a link between Kelley and the mystery man," I said. "Otherwise, why would they both be under scrutiny from the same DOJ investigation?"

"But wait. We know Kelley was working with Nora."

"Yes. That's right."

"And Nora ordered the hit on Dimitrovsky," Mary said. "Then — "

"Hold it for a second. Nora gave me the order for Dimitrovsky. But she doesn't make those decisions on her own."

"You mean, she's not supposed to make them on her own, don't you?"

"You're right. What else are you thinking?"

"When she assigned you the mission, you thought it was government-sanctioned, didn't you?"

"Yes. But now I doubt that."

"I see why," Mary said. "I've been working on the assumption that Nora was acting for O'Hanlon, but why would O'Hanlon want Dimitrovsky killed?"

"Good question. Maybe he saw him as a competitor. Dimitrovsky was smuggling drugs to bankroll his other operation."

"Okay. That could be. Phorcys sent me to make sure that nobody interfered with your hit. That means they thought somebody might. You with me so far?"

"So far," I said. "Go ahead."

"From what you and I saw, it looked like Frankie Dailey was the one trying to stop you. You agree?"

"Well, he told me the three men who jumped us in Puerto Real were working for him," I said. "And the three people who attacked you in Bequia. But are you sure they were looking for me and not you?"

"As far as any of them knew when they attacked, I was just some girl you picked up along the way, remember?"

"That's right. Okay, so you think Frankie was trying to stop me from killing Dimitrovsky."

"Yes. It looks that way to me. Not to you?"

"Well, it does, but it doesn't square with the idea that Frankie was working for O'Hanlon," I said.

"No. But Frankie double-crossed his own parents. Tortured and killed them. Seems loyalty was not his strongest trait," Mary said. "He did that to his own parents; O'Hanlon was only his uncle."

"You're saying he double-crossed O'Hanlon, too?"

"That's the way it looks," she said. "But then who was giving Frankie his orders?"

"Dimitrovsky was working for Russia," I said. "That's not much of a stretch; he was funding the lunatic fringe at both ends of the political spectrum, making all kinds of trouble in the States."

"Are you saying Frankie was part of the Russian operation Aaron was hinting at?" she asked.

"He might not have known it. Or maybe he did. But you just said he didn't have any loyalty to anybody."

"Except himself," Mary said. "He was an ambitious bastard."

"What makes you say that?"

"Stuff I overheard when he was grilling his parents."

"Okay. That makes him a good candidate for manipulation by our mystery man."

"I agree," Mary said.

"Yes. But even though Aaron said there might be several Russian agents at work here, one of them is bound to be in charge. That's our mystery man. The others are just his troops."

"This all fits together, Finn. If Frankie was selling out O'Hanlon to the Russians, it makes sense that they might use him to protect Dimitrovsky, don't you think?"

"Yes. And if O'Hanlon already had a bunch of high-level politicians in his pocket, it makes sense that the Russians would want to take over his game. Ready to talk about Phorcys?"

"Sure, but do you think we could open another bottle of wine?"

"You bet," I said.

32

MARY SIPPED HER WINE AND LISTENED WITHOUT COMMENT AS I told her what Aaron learned about Phorcys. A frown creased her face when I mentioned the special operations group.

"Does that ring a bell or something?" I asked.

"No," she said, "but it makes me wonder why they would hire somebody like me, if they have that kind of talent in-house."

"Aaron didn't say they had the talent in-house. Could be that's the part of the organization that hired you."

"Maybe," she said. "Sorry to interrupt. You were about to tell me what he said about the senator's suicide."

I watched for a reaction as I told her about the three alibi witnesses who disappeared. She gave no sign that she knew anything about it. But that didn't mean much. She fooled me several times before.

Even though we were being more open with one another, that wasn't the kind of thing people like us talked about. I wasn't surprised that she kept her own counsel, but I decided to press my luck.

"Was that what you were doing while I was sailing back and forth to St. Martin? Cleaning up after Phorcys?"

She looked me in the eye, hesitating before she answered. "Yes. I would have told you, but it didn't seem to matter. Does it?"

"No, I don't think it matters. But I wondered. Did they call you about it, or did you figure it out yourself? That it needed to be done, I mean."

"They called. Actually, they called before the mistress went to the cops. Whoever set up the bogus backstory on the senator realized the vulnerability at the time they set it up. They had planned to fix it somehow before they used the backstory. Maybe bribes to the witnesses — I don't know. But once she went to the cops, there was only one possible solution."

"What happened that caused them to miss that problem with the witnesses?"

"We rushed them. That's my guess, anyway. Pushed them into it before they could get the fix in. As best I can tell, they were planning to leak the dirt to force the senator to resign. They weren't going to do away with him until we came along. But then we decided to kill him."

"Did they have a problem with that?"

"With our deciding to kill him, you mean?"

"Yes. With that."

"No. Not since he was involved in the kidnapping. Once he did that, they would have probably hit him on their own. But my contact said it was our call, anyway. They wouldn't have second-guessed us. But until then, they weren't sure he was anything more than a typical scumbag politician. So they would have ruined him, but not killed him."

"You're saying they would have killed him on their own?

Once they found out he engineered the kidnapping, I mean?"

"I don't know for sure, but that was the implication."

"I want to ask more questions about your work for them, but I don't want to piss you off, or embarrass you."

"Okay. Ask. I'll do my best."

"I understand if you don't want to answer. I'm just trying to figure out what Phorcys is all about. My questions are about them, not about you."

"I said okay, Finn. Whatever you need to ask, I'll answer. If it ruins things between us, I'll have to live with that. I know what I've done; I have to live with it all. You don't."

She held my gaze, waiting, a grim look on her face.

"The other jobs you did for them," I asked, "were they hits?"

"Most of them, yes. But a few times, they needed somebody to — "

"It's the hits I want to talk about. I don't need to know about other stuff."

I watched as her face relaxed.

"Okay. What about the hits?"

"Aaron seemed to imply that they only put out contracts on traitors, and then only the ones that the government wouldn't prosecute. How does that square with your experience?"

"One hundred percent. But that's only my deals. I guess maybe they have other people like me. I don't know. But the people I killed, they deserved it. You know where I draw the line."

I nodded. "Thanks for leveling with me. You're a brave woman."

"Brave?" Her brow wrinkled. "I don't see that, Finn."

"Trust me. I see it."

She looked at me for several seconds, then nodded. "Thanks. I needed that. Is there more about Phorcys?"

"You mean from Aaron?"

"Yes."

"No. That's about it. At least so far. He's got a source that seems to know a lot about them. He said that she thinks they can do no wrong."

"Even though they kill people? When I listened to you telling me what Aaron said, Phorcys sounded like a vigilante group. Who is this woman? His source?"

I shook my head. "I have no idea. I don't want to know. But she's probably one of us."

"One of us? What do you mean by that?"

"Somebody that lives by their own rules. Somebody with an Old Testament sense of morality. Somebody who thinks vigilantes have their place."

"One of us, you said. You think you and I are that way?"

"You know damn well we are."

"Then why am I so ashamed of the things I've done, Finn?"

"I don't know. My guess is that you think you need approval from somebody you see as an authority figure."

"And you don't?"

I shook my head. "Once you've been around a while, you realize the people in authority are no different than we are. The honest ones, anyway. There are always a few who're full of shit, claim they know better than the rest of us. But they don't. We all screw up every so often. The best we can do is try to do what's right. We fall short sometimes. Get used to it."

"I'm trying."

"Good. Keep the faith. You know right from wrong; trust your judgment."

"I love you, Finn."

"I know. And that makes me the luckiest man alive. I love you, too. But there's one other thing we need to talk about before we get all mushy."

"What's that?"

"I have to call Nora tomorrow."

"Oh, yeah. That," she said.

"That, indeed."

"Are you worried about it?"

"Not particularly, but I need to have an idea of how to play it."

"You said the boss was going to give her orders to kill you."

"Yes. That's what he said."

"So what's the problem?" Mary asked.

"The problem is I don't want her to do that. I had a different outcome in mind."

That got a smile from Mary, which pleased me. I didn't like her being somber. "But her boss said he would sandbag her, didn't he? Fix it so her backup would turn her over to you?"

"We both know that's bullshit," I said. "They're setting me up. You, too."

"So that makes it simple," she said. "You need to let her lead you into the trap, that's all. She'll think she's got the upper hand. Just play along with her."

"Right. But she's going to need to be face-to-face with me."

"Why's that a problem?" Mary asked.

"She thinks we're in the Bahamas."

"Oh, yeah. I forgot that. And she knows I'm with you. Assuming somebody saw us together in Guánica and lived to tell her."

"That's a safe bet," I said. "There was somebody there besides the two idiots who lusted after you and my laptop."

"We're what, five or six hundred miles from where that tracker says we are?"

"That's right."

"And we could make 100 to 120 miles a day, so that's five days, roughly. Is that too long? Will she be in a hurry?"

"Guaranteed, she'll be in a hurry. What's going on in that devious mind of yours, Mary?"

"Just weighing the options. What if you made her think you were spooked?"

"Spooked?"

"Scared of her; suspicious that she's up to no good," Mary said. "Could you bring that off?"

"I don't know. Probably. Why?"

"The tracker's been sitting still for 24 hours, now, right?"

"Yes. So?" I frowned.

"So, what are the chances they're already moving on us?"

"Shit, I didn't think of that. Probably good. Say they spent several hours getting their act together and then started moving. They would probably use go-fast boats."

"Could they have discovered we're not where the tracker puts us?" Mary asked.

"Maybe. I don't know. They could have, especially if they used a spotter plane."

"Where did you put us? Some deserted island?"

"No. I had a wild notion that since we were really going to

an uninhabited island, I would put us in the middle of a crowd." I laughed. "Just my perverse nature, I guess. The tracker thinks we're anchored in Georgetown, in the Exumas."

"I don't know the Bahamas well. Georgetown's crowded, I gather?"

"This time of year, it is. There're probably several hundred cruising boats there. They'll have a tough time discovering we're not there."

She grinned. "You're pretty sneaky. What if you shut off the tracker? Can you do that?"

"Sure. I can just yank the batteries."

"Yes. Like that. So they'll think it broke."

I chuckled. "That'll confuse them, all right. But it doesn't solve my problem with Nora."

"No. But it can't hurt. You're worried about where to meet her, right?"

"That's right. Any thoughts?"

"Yes. This is supposed to be her party, right? Not yours."

"Right. So?"

"So, let her pick the place."

"She'll pick somewhere close to Georgetown," I said.

"Then tell her that's a five-day sail for you. See how she reacts. Negotiate a different spot, maybe. If you could pick a place to meet her and the assassin, where would it be?"

"Good question. I've been struggling with that. Either crowded or deserted. Nothing in between."

Mary nodded. "Crowded would favor us more. Deserted would let them pick us off from a distance. I figure they'll be better equipped, with weapons and such. Right?"

"Probably."

"How will they feel about collateral damage?"

"You mean innocent bystanders?"

"Yes."

"They won't like that," I said. "They want to keep a low profile. Plus, they'll want to disable us and then interrogate us."

"Then a densely populated area would give us more protection. That's what I'd pick. Maybe even an airport, or a ferry terminal. Somewhere with cops."

"How will we turn the tables on them, then?" I asked.

"Distract her backup and drug Nora. I'd guess drugs are easier to come by than weapons are, most places down here."

"Yes. With ship's papers, I can walk in a pharmacy and buy anything we need in the way of drugs."

"Really? Why ship's papers?"

"Under international law, the captain of a vessel can stock any medication in the ship's stores. And pharmacists in seaports know that."

"Then we have the makings of a plan," Mary said. "Since she knows you, you can be the bait to attract Nora, and I'll hang back and take care of her backup. Once they're out of action, we'll dope her up and pretend she's drunk. Lead her away and work on her. What do you think?"

"Like you said, the makings of a plan," I said. "Good enough for now, anyway."

"Anything else we need to work through?" Mary asked. "I'm about ready to call it a night."

"One thing. Aaron wanted me to check the blind drop this evening; he thought he might have something on the DOJ and the Russians."

I powered up the hotspot and connected the laptop, finding a message from Aaron.

"Mind if I read over your shoulder?" Mary asked.

"Be my guest," I said, opening the message.

URGENT!!! Call ASAP! You are in immediate danger.

"Not what I was expecting," I said, deleting the draft. "Can you hand me my phone?"

33

"WHAT DO YOU MEAN, 'IN IMMEDIATE DANGER?'" I ASKED, WHEN Aaron answered my call.

My phone was set to speaker mode, and Mary was listening.

"Thank God you got my message," Aaron said. "I'm relieved that you're okay. I'm not sure how long you have."

Mary's eyes were like saucers. I put my hand over the phone's microphone and raised my eyebrows, inviting her to speak.

She shook her head and gestured for me to continue.

"How long I have? Before what?" I asked. "What are you talking about?"

"They're coming for you; you need to get the hell out of Georgetown, right now!"

Now it was my turn to look surprised. Mary's expression had changed. Leaning toward me, she cupped my ear. "Don't tell him where we are."

I nodded. "Georgetown?"

"They put a tracker on your boat; they know you're in the

Exumas. They've already dispatched a team to take you out. Is the girl with you?"

Mary shook her head vigorously.

"I've got things under control, Aaron. But who put a tracker on the boat? Nora?"

"I don't think so, but I wouldn't rule it out. You sure you're safe? My information is almost a day old; they could be watching you right now."

"I'm a long way from Georgetown. Where did you pick this up?"

"I told you about the super-secret DOJ investigation into the Russians, remember?"

"Yes. But — "

"My source got into the DOJ's system. They have telephone intercepts on the suspected Russian agents. She downloaded them and combed through them."

"And found out about me?"

"She doesn't know who you are, but she knows I'm following certain kinds of activity in the islands. What she found was a reference to a boat one of the suspects was tracking from Puerto Rico. The boat came to rest in Georgetown a day ago. He called another one of them about it, and the second one ordered him to capture the man and the woman aboard and get the files. You're saying that wasn't you?"

I raised my eyebrows and looked at Mary. She shrugged.

"Yes and no," I said. "I found the tracker and spoofed it."

"You sly bastard. Good for you. They saw you pick up the girl and take her back to the boat in some place called Guánica. The first guy said the two locals he hired to plant the tracker disappeared before he could pay them. The DOJ team's trying to get a line on the two locals."

"Uh-huh," I said. "Thanks for the tip."

"You're not in Guánica now, are you?"

"Nope. Long gone."

"Good. No point in getting mixed up with the DOJ if you can help it."

"Right," I said. "As long as I've got you on the line, did you find out anything else about the Russians?"

"She's still working it. There's one of them who's in charge, and you called it. He's been ordered to take over O'Hanlon's network of crooked politicians. His mission's to cause political chaos, besides fueling the drug and human trafficking problems we've already got. And he's going to line his pockets — and Putin's. DOJ's got him pegged as one of the richest of Putin's crooked cronies, but if they have a name for him, they're keeping it under wraps. That's about all we've got, so far."

"How about on the files?"

"Nothing new there. We're trying to find the source of the cyberattack, so we can block 'em and get back to work."

"Okay. Thanks for looking out for me."

"No problem, man. It's the least I can do. Glad you're out of harm's way on this one."

"Me, too."

"Keep an eye on the email drop. There's no good way for me to call you, right?"

"No, there isn't. I'll check the drop often, though. Thanks again, and stay well."

Once we disconnected, Mary broke her silence. "Just to confirm," she said, "that was your friend Aaron?"

"Yes. Why do you ask?"

"I recognized his voice."

That sent a chill down my spine. "From where?"

"A recording. I heard it during a briefing for a hit; there was a snippet of audio. There were two men talking about the target; your friend was one."

"And the other?"

She shook her head. "No clue, but I definitely recognize Aaron's voice."

"Who was the client, Mary?"

"I don't know. I told you how the bookings work — double blind. I know the target, but not who's paying me."

"Then who was the target?"

"A nobody, I thought at the time. A scummy bastard named Jimmy Harris. He was a small-time trafficker, pimping out these girls he bought from the coyotes that brought them in. Worked in central Florida."

"You thought he was a nobody *at the time*, you say?"

She nodded, chewing on her lower lip.

"You feel differently now? Is that it?"

She shook her head, frowning. "I don't know what to think, Finn. He was a small-time operator, as best I knew. But a nasty piece of shit. How does that square with somebody like Aaron being involved with him? To me, that doesn't make sense."

"I agree," I said. "Not on the face of it, anyhow. You remember Aaron's voice; can you remember what he said?"

"Not really; it was more like the other man was briefing him, describing Harris, the target, talking about where he usually hung out, how many women he was running, where they worked. That kind of stuff. So Aaron was mostly asking questions, leading the other guy along."

"When was this? How long ago?"

"Well, I can't say exactly. But it would have been maybe

two years, give or take. Not long after that hit, I got my first assignment from Phorcys."

"Why does that fix the timing in your mind?"

"It was one of the last of those double-blind deals. And it was like a threshold job for me; my first big payoff."

"The last of the double-blind deals? You don't do those anymore?"

"I do, but not often. Phorcys has kept me busy. I told you, my work with them has reached the point where there's enough trust that we skip the double-blind business. They book directly with me, now."

"What about the broker?"

"Oh, she still gets her cut; they pass the money through her. But it's a better deal for all of us. There's a lot less overhead work for me and for her, because Phorcys is so well organized."

"I'm not sure what you mean by that."

"They've done most of the homework before they come to me. Plus, they pay better than most clients."

"Do you take on other clients?"

"Yes, but why do you ask?"

"Curious. I'm trying to fit Aaron into that picture."

"I do take other work. But not often. I don't have much incentive to take the other jobs since I connected with Phorcys. Sometimes I'll do one, but it's mostly as a favor to the broker when she's in a bind. I don't want to burn any bridges."

"I understand. I don't know what to make of the Aaron thing."

"It set off alarms, Finn. It was a surprise. That's all. I have no idea where that client got the recording, or whether they had more than I heard. I just thought I should mention it."

"Yes; you were right about that. But I don't think there's much point in obsessing over it now."

"Okay. There's this Russian business he brought up, though," Mary said. "What do you think of that?"

"I'm not sure, but that reminds me; I should go ahead and kill that tracker. What do you think?"

"I agree. They're going to discover they've been had pretty soon. Then they'll probably start over in Guánica, looking for us."

We went up on deck and I opened the life raft valise, taking out the tracker and the GPS spoofer. Mary closed the valise, and I took the two devices below deck.

Putting the two of them on the chart table, I got out my set of jeweler's screwdrivers and opened the tracker. After I disconnected the battery, I shut off the spoofer and returned it to the hiding place under the charts.

"What are we going to do with it," Mary asked, looking at the tracking device.

"Once we get back into deep water, we'll toss it over the side."

"We can't reuse it?"

"Not easily. You need the web address of the site where you can retrieve its location, plus a user name and password. Besides, I picked up a couple of new ones in St. Martin if we need one."

"That's my guy," Mary said. "Always thinking ahead. Speaking of which, do you have any more thoughts on how to deal with Nora tomorrow?"

"I've consulted with a person who specializes in knowing how sneaky, devious women think," I said. "That kind of thing is way over my poor, testosterone-addled head. I'm going to take the consultant's advice and let Nora lead the way."

"I'm surprised you know anyone like that consultant, Finn."

"I'd be lost without her guidance."

"Uh-huh. I think it's time to call it a night before you get in trouble. How about you?"

"If you say it's time, it's time. No arguments from me."

34

"WHEN ARE YOU GOING TO CALL HER?" MARY ASKED.

We were in the cockpit, drinking the last of our coffee from breakfast.

"They're an hour behind us; it's a little too early. And I'm supposed to call the boss, first."

"You didn't tell me that."

"Sorry. It's not a big deal; I need to make sure he's prepped her. That's all."

"His idea? Or yours?"

"The call? His idea. They're all control freaks, those desk jockeys."

Mary smiled. "Yeah, well, I guess I can see why. It's not like they're doing anything themselves. That would drive me nuts, being hands-off like they are."

"That's why you're doing what you do."

"On a different subject, Finn, I'm sad that we're going to be leaving this spot. I feel like I wasted yesterday, spending it all by myself."

"You needed that. Besides, we're not gone yet. We'll have to see where Nora wants to meet. And when."

"Now that you've had time to think about it, where would you pick, Finn? To meet her, if she left it up to you?"

"Maybe Bourg de Saintes."

"That's in Guadeloupe, right?"

"That's right."

"Why there? The French police are thorough, compared to other places down here."

"True. But Bourg des Saintes is an odd place. I think there's one cop there; he handles mostly customs clearance for yachts. Maybe there are a few more policemen. A few more, but not many. It's not a big place, but it's a tourist trap. The main access from Guadeloupe is by ferry. When the tourists come off the ferry, it's a mob scene. They mill around like a bunch of sheep. If we knew she was coming in that way, it would be easy to spot her and her backup."

"And cut them out of the herd?" Mary asked. "Or flock, I guess it would be, with sheep."

"Well, the reason to cut them out of the flock would be so we could interrogate her. But I'm wondering if we should bother with that, now."

"She might give us a line on who this Russian is," Mary said.

"Yes. She might. That's the only worthwhile thing I can think of that she might know. We could still interrogate her, though. We could shoot her up with roofies like they did Abby and lead her to the dinghy. In the mob that forms when the ferry lands, anybody who noticed would just think she was another drunken tourist."

"What about her backup?" Mary asked.

"She may have a heart attack, right in the middle of the crowd."

"A heart attack?" Mary asked.

"Potassium chloride injection," I said.

"That'll just drop her in her tracks? Right in the crowd?" she asked.

"Yes. All you'll need to do is inject her and get clear. It's quick."

"Can we get the stuff we need there? In Bourg des Saintes?" Mary asked.

"It's already in the ship's medicine chest. Syringes and roofies. The potassium chloride's in the galley, pretending to be a salt substitute."

"And how far a sail is Bourg des Saintes?"

"Only 120 miles, but it's almost due east."

"Straight into the wind," Mary said. "But we could do that in 24 hours, give or take."

"Yep. But that's only if Nora's okay with meeting in the Saintes. It's late enough now; I'll try the boss."

"Mind if I eavesdrop?" Mary asked.

"I was planning on it."

The laptop and the hotspot were already in the cockpit. I went below and retrieved the phone while Mary got everything up and running. After I went through the authentication routine, the boss said, "She's all primed. You still on board?"

"Yes," I said.

"She wants to do this down in the islands. That work for you?"

"Sure. But remember, I can't move all that fast."

"There are planes and airports."

"Yes, but the schedules aren't what you might be used to,

and I'm a long way from an airport right now."

"Where are you?"

"I'm within striking distance of several good-sized islands. Think she's going to be flexible about the location?"

"She should be, as long as you stay outside U.S. territory. Do you need for me to nudge her in a certain direction?"

"I'll let you know," I said.

"Good enough. Let's get this done; I've got work for you to do once she's out of the way."

"Yes, sir. Looking forward to it."

"Call me when it's finished, unless you need something before then." He disconnected.

"Shit, Finn. I can't believe this," Mary said.

"What?"

"That's the other guy from the recording. He was the one briefing Aaron on that hit I told you about last night."

"You sure?"

"Yes. He was giving Aaron all the skinny on that Jimmy Harris character."

I thought about that for several seconds. Mary held my gaze, a worried look on her face.

"You killed him, right?" I asked.

She nodded. "Why?"

"Trying to fit the pieces together. I wish you knew who ordered the hit. I know you don't, but..."

"What are you thinking, Finn?"

"Whoever it was, they knew about Aaron. Somebody who had access to that recorded conversation between Aaron and Nora's boss."

"Did you and Aaron ever discuss Nora's boss?"

"Only in passing. Why?"

"Do you think he might know the boss's identity?"

"It's possible. If Aaron wanted to know, he could have discovered it, I'm sure. There isn't much information that's safe from Aaron."

"Would he share that with you?"

"Yes, if I asked point blank. And if he knew."

"Would you trust his answer?"

"Yes. Unless..."

"Unless what?" she asked.

"Unless he gave me a reason not to. Why?"

"I think you should ask him."

"About Nora's boss? Why?"

"Well, not just about that. About Jimmy Harris, too."

I mulled that over for several seconds. "Maybe so. I'm not sure it changes anything, as far as Nora goes."

"No," Mary said. "I didn't think it would. I'm looking down the road; her boss is our next target. Right?"

"He's definitely on the list," I said.

"There's no reason to wait, is there?" she asked.

"You mean to wait to ask Aaron?"

"Right."

"Not that I can see. You think I should call him before I call Nora?"

"What can it hurt? More information's always good, isn't it?"

"I reckon. Let's see what Aaron remembers about Jimmy Harris." I keyed the number for Aaron's latest burner phone into my iPhone.

35

"I've got a question for you," I said, when Aaron answered. "It doesn't go back as far as Elena, but it's a trip down memory lane, just the same." I wanted to make sure he had time to recognize my voice.

"Okay. Ask away."

"You ever get any background on a person named Jimmy Harris?"

"Jimmy Harris," Aaron said. "What brought you to ask about him?"

"His name came up in conversation with my friend. He was some kind of lowlife in central Florida, and we wondered if he was connected to... let's just say, one of the people we dealt with recently."

"If he was, it would have been a while back." Aaron said. "Somebody punched his ticket a couple of years ago. But he could have been connected to that person who died of the accidental overdose recently. He was in the same line of business. And I don't mean politics."

"Mind telling me what you know about him?"

Aaron was silent for several seconds. "I can do that. But what I know is limited. We were checking him out in connection with a drug-smuggling ring that was funding some ugly people from one of those countries where you and I used to work. You with me so far?"

"Yes." Aaron's oblique reference was to Middle-Eastern terrorists. "I'm following so far."

"It turned out he wasn't involved with them, but he was still a vile bastard. Nora had me work up a profile on him before we decided he wasn't of interest to us. She hooked me up with an anonymous source who knew a lot about Harris. I had a phone call or two with him. I remember picking his brain, but I don't know who he was or where she found him."

"And what happened with the information?"

"I consolidated everything we had. Put together one of our normal dossiers on him. The next thing I heard was that somebody blew him away. It appeared to be a typical drug-related hit; could have been one of his competitors. As far as I know, that was nothing to do with us."

"So he was dealing?"

"Small time. His main thing was women; he was heavily into pimping. But drugs are part of that whole scene. You know that. And that's about all I can tell you. Does that help?"

I looked at Mary before I answered. She shook her head and shrugged.

"I think so. Sounds like he was gone before any of the stuff we're working on happened. Thanks anyway."

"Sure, man. No problem. I'll be in touch on the other things. Stay safe."

"You, too," I said, and disconnected the call.

"Do you trust what he told you?" Mary asked.

"As far as it went, yes. But I think he knew more. He wasn't going to volunteer it, and I didn't want to push him on something that may not matter to us. He didn't think it was relevant to what we're into, or he would have been more forthcoming. I can always go back to him later if need be. What's your reaction?"

"It sounds like Nora was putting together the file on the guy, from what Aaron said. And she set her boss up as an anonymous source for Aaron. That's weird. Why would she have done that?"

"She and her boss wanted this Harris out of the picture. Or maybe just her boss did, and farmed it out to Nora. She got Aaron to put together one of our standard target profiles and then told Aaron that Harris wasn't the sort of target she was hunting."

"But why would she have done that?"

"It could have been to cover their tracks. She got the dossier from Aaron and told him 'thanks, but it was a false alarm.' Or something like that. Then she passed the dossier on to someone else, who put out the contract on Harris."

"But who would that have been?"

"The senator comes to mind. Harris might have been stepping on his toes, somehow. Or some of the O'Hanlon crowd."

"What about the recording, though? Would that have been a normal thing?"

"I don't know," I said. "But Aaron might have recorded an interview with an anonymous source. When I got briefed on targets, I sometimes got snippets of interviews like that. It avoids losing nuanced information — little things that could get lost in transcription. But it wouldn't normally ever be heard by anybody outside our organization."

Mary nodded. "You're still talking like you're one of them, Finn."

"I am?"

"You used the phrase, 'outside our organization.'"

"You're right. Old habits die hard, I guess. I don't feel like one of them. Not anymore."

"This is off the subject, Finn, but I have to wonder who paid me to hit Harris."

"You said it was anonymous — through your broker."

"It was. But I..." She shook her head, frowning.

"That's a distraction, Mary. You'll never know. Could have even been Nora. Or the senator, or O'Hanlon. Or somebody we never heard of, who had hooks into Nora."

She thought about that for a few seconds, frowning. Then she nodded.

"You ready to call Nora?" she asked.

"Yes," I said, keying the number into the iPhone.

36

Nora answered, rattling off the four-digit code I used to get past the first menu.

"Sorry for the delayed response," I said. "I haven't been where I could get email. I just got your message. What's up?"

She waited for a cue from her voice recognition system.

"Okay, you're authenticated," she said, after a few seconds. "Are you on a clean phone?"

"VOIP through a VPN, via a satellite connection."

"That should do it. What happened to the satellite phone I gave you?"

"Stolen," I said, skipping the details I gave her boss the day before. I was curious to see what she said, versus what I told him.

"I wondered. It was found in the Miami airport, not long after you and I talked. Did somebody snatch it while you were waiting on your flight back to the islands?"

That's at odds with what I told your boss yesterday. A couple of possibilities here. You lied to me about the phone's tracking being disabled, or you made a guess and tossed it out, to see if I would give away anything.

"They stole it while I was in the bar. Druggies, probably. My guess is they hocked it to buy dope." Her boss would have told her about his conversation with me. If she was trying to trip me up and get me to admit I was in Miami, my answer didn't give her any help. Or she lied, and she had tracking data that put me in Miami when she talked with me a few days ago.

"Whoever stole it sanitized it for you," she said.

I didn't respond.

"Pulled the SIM and everything. I figured you did that and ditched it."

She's messing with me; she knows I'm not going to take the bait. She's up to something, here. But what?

"Why would I have done that?"

"I thought you were worried after what happened in St. Thomas. Not that I would blame you. It *was* a little strange."

"Yes, it was. But somebody just took the phone while I wasn't looking." *Even if she had tracking data from the sat phone, she couldn't know where in the airport I was when we spoke. Unless she had somebody on the ground watching me.*

"Could be, I guess. They must have been pissed when they discovered they stole a phone that didn't work," she said.

"Maybe that's why they stripped it," I said.

"Maybe. The girl still with you?"

"I can reach her if I need to. Why?"

Mary grinned and poked me in the ribs.

"I just wondered."

Was Nora behind planting the tracker in Guánica? If so, she knows Mary's with me. How can I test that?

"She called from Florida," I said.

"So she's there now?" Nora asked.

"She could be, I guess."

"Do you know where in Florida?"

"No, not really. She was visiting family. Different places, I think."

Is she screwing with me? Or does she not know Mary came to Puerto Rico? And what about the tracker planted on Island Girl? Wouldn't the Russians tell her, if she works for them?

"You and I need to meet again, Finn. Face-to-face. A lot's going on."

I didn't say anything, waiting to see what she proposed.

"You're in the islands?" she asked.

"Yes. You going to come down?"

"I can do that. Where's a good place for you? St. Martin again? It's easy for me to get there."

"I could do that. Depends on how soon, though. That's two days of hard sailing, if the wind holds. How about somewhere farther south?"

"Like where?"

"I could be in the Saintes pretty quick."

"In Guadeloupe?" she asked.

"Yes, that's right."

"Hang on a sec," she said. I could hear her keyboard clicking as she checked the flights. "Hmm. That sucks. One flight a day. Unless... okay. I'll spend a night in Miami. That's not too bad. I can get some work done there. That puts me in Pointe-à-Pitre day after tomorrow. How do I get to the Saintes?"

"There are plenty of ferries and nice places to stay. I'd figure on spending the night in the Saintes. I'll meet you for dinner, maybe?"

"Yes. I'm looking... okay. You're on. Do you still have that iPhone?"

"No — "

Mary poked me and leaned over to cup my ear. "Hang on a sec. I've got an unused burner. Let me get the number." She scrambled down the companionway ladder.

"Just a second, Nora. I'm looking for my prepaid local phone."

"Okay. I've booked my flights, working on lodging. Looks like several nice places."

Mary handed me a scrap of paper with a Martinique cellphone number. I read it off to Nora, and she repeated it to me.

"That's it," I said.

"Good. I'll call you when I'm leaving the airport. Do you look the same as the last time I saw you?"

"Yes."

"Good. I'll find you. You won't recognize me. But you'll like my new look. I've been thinking about that um...business we didn't get around to in St. Martin." She made a kissing sound. "Bring your toothbrush." With that, she disconnected the call.

"Bring your toothbrush?" Mary laughed. "I'm just imagining the *business* you two *didn't get around to in St. Martin.* She's your age?"

"Give or take. Why?"

"I don't know. Just her choice of words. That was supposed to get you thinking about a romantic interlude?"

"I can't imagine what else she was hinting at," I said. "She was flirting with me in St. Martin."

"Can't blame her for that." Mary laughed again and shook her head. "Old people."

"Hey, kid, watch who you're calling old."

"Think you can run with the young dogs, old man?"

"Try me."

"You're on, but you have to catch me first." She slipped off the T-shirt she slept in. "Bring your toothbrush." She laughed and dove over the side, striking out for the beach. I was right behind her, but I let her get to the shallow water before I caught her.

37

WHEN THE FERRY FROM GUADELOUPE ROUNDED ÎLET À CABRIT two days later, I was standing in the back of the crowd of vendors waiting to hustle the late afternoon arrivals. Mary called me an hour earlier to tell me she spotted Nora and her companion when they got to the ferry terminal in Pointe-à-Pitre.

Mary and I arrived in Bourg des Saintes early the previous afternoon and scouted the area. *Island Girl* was anchored by herself, tucked in behind Tête Rouge, off Anse Galet. That was a half a mile from town, but well away from the crowds of visiting yachts in the more popular anchorages.

This morning, Mary caught an early ferry from Bourg des Saintes to Pointe-à-Pitre to stake out the ferry terminal there. Although she only had my description of Nora to go on, she didn't have any trouble spotting the two women. Obvious American tourists with little command of French, they stuck out among the crowd of locals and Europeans on holiday.

Wearing a baseball cap, ragged designer jeans, and a tie-dyed T-shirt, Mary looked like a typical young Eurotrash vagabond. Even if Nora saw her in St. Thomas when Mary killed the crooked FBI agent, she wouldn't recognize her today.

My throwaway cellphone vibrated against my thigh. I pulled it from my pocket and checked to be sure it was Mary calling.

"Hey," I said.

"Hey, yourself. We're just rounding the point into the harbor."

"Yes, I see you."

"They've split up, getting ready to go ashore separately. Nora looks good. She cleans up nice. You'll spot her, with the big straw hat and the gauzy white wraparound skirt. She's wearing a matching bikini top and a spray-on tan. Truck-stop blond hair — lots of it. Definitely on the make. You behave yourself with her, you hear?"

"Yes, ma'am. I'll restrain myself. What about the hitter?"

"I've got her. Nothing remarkable at all. Attractive and neatly dressed, but not flashy. Fades into the background. You have to look twice to be sure she's really even there. She's good, I'll bet."

"You nervous? Going up against another pro?"

"Scared to death. I was sitting right behind them before they separated. They're clueless. You just deal with Nora. I'll put Miss Nondescript away and join you as quickly as I can. Think you can keep Nora on her feet until we get her to the dinghy?"

"I'll manage."

"I'm sure. Better go. The captain's slowing this thing down. I need to get in position. Bye."

I put the phone back in my pocket and made a last-minute check on the syringe taped to the inside of my left forearm. The sheath over the needle was fastened securely, but the barrel and plunger were held loosely. It was hidden by the long sleeve of the loose-fitting fishing shirt I wore.

Satisfied, I moved away from the crowd a little, hoping to make myself easy for Nora to spot. Besides, I wanted to be sure nobody was close enough to see what happened, in case things didn't go smoothly.

The ferry's rusted steel hull ground against the rough concrete of the pier. Two deck hands dropped mooring lines over the bollards, and the skipper throttled the engines back to idle.

When the gangway clanked into place, Nora was one of the first ashore. Thanks to Mary, I recognized her with no problem. I chuckled at the memory of Mary's catty description. No wonder. Nora was drop-dead gorgeous. *Dressed to kill. Me.*

She paused before she reached the front rank of vendors. Slinging her soft leather travel bag over her shoulder, she rose to tiptoes and scanned the crowd.

Just before Nora spotted me, I saw a disturbance on the ferry's bridge. An agitated crewman scrambled up the ladder and went inside the wheelhouse. Seconds later, he emerged, followed by two men in officer's uniforms. They stepped out onto the side deck, one carrying a large yellow bag with a big red cross on it. The crewman led them down a ladder at a fast clip, and they disappeared from view.

Mary stepped off the gangway onto the dock, ambling toward the vendors as she gawked at the sights like the rest of the people on holiday. She must have accomplished her mission.

Returning my attention to Nora, I stood still. I pretended to watch the people coming off the ferry, remembering that I wasn't supposed to recognize her. And without Mary's warning, I wouldn't have noticed Nora, except perhaps to admire her stunning good looks.

When she saw me, her face lit up with a thousand-watt smile and she walked straight toward me. When she broke from the crowd, she called out, "Hi, handsome!"

I returned the smile and gave her a little wave. "Welcome to the Saintes," I said. "You look wonderful."

"Aw, you're sweet to say so." She dropped her shoulder bag and stepped into my arms.

As I returned her embrace, I looked over her shoulder to make sure no one was watching us. Mary was. She was moving at a leisurely pace, coming toward us. When she caught my eye, she smirked and shook her head.

Nora wrapped both arms around my neck and shoulders, turning her face up for a kiss. I tipped my head down and obliged. As her kiss became progressively more passionate, my hands stroked the bare skin of her lower back. When her tongue found its way past my lips, I squeezed her hip with my left hand, moaning a little to encourage her.

I could feel the edge of her bikini bottoms through the flimsy fabric of her skirt; the back of the bottoms wasn't quite a thong, but it was close enough for my purposes. I slid my right hand down and pulled her tighter against me as I unbuttoned the left cuff of my long-sleeved shirt. While I massaged her bottom with my left hand, I took the syringe in my right. Plunging it through the gauzy skirt into her bare left hip, I tightened my left arm, keeping my mouth over hers as she struggled briefly. As I felt Nora relax, Mary tapped me on the shoulder. No longer kissing me, Nora put her head on my chest, snuggling against me.

"Enough, you pervert. Unhand that poor woman. You're taking advantage of her. I saw you groping her."

Nora mumbled something unintelligible, leaning against me. Her face was split in a goofy grin, and her gaze was unfocused.

"She was loving every second of it," I said.

"You need counseling, you old reprobate," Mary said. "And I'm going to show you what consent means. But first..."

Mary took Nora's left arm from around my neck and ducked under it, taking part of Nora's weight. I took Nora's other arm, draped it over my shoulders, and put my left arm around her waist. As we took our first step, I leaned down and scooped up Nora's bag in my right hand.

"Shall we go for a nice little sail?" Mary asked.

"Sailing, sailing, over the bounding... what's it?" Nora gurgled, as we led her to the dinghy.

38

Several hours later, *Island Girl* was rolling along, running before a brisk 20-knot breeze. I was on watch, and Mary was below cooking dinner. Our course was to the west; Mary wanted to spend more time at Isla de Aves. I was all for that.

Nora wasn't with us any longer. We dropped her overboard about 45 minutes earlier, with a little anchor chain to take her to the bottom in about 4,000 feet of water. She answered our questions readily enough. The drugs Mary administered made Nora downright chatty.

We learned that Nora's boss, Henry Jacobs, was Deputy Undersecretary of Defense for Political Studies. She was quick to tell us we wouldn't find that information — not even his title — on any public documents. She also volunteered that Henry was her lover.

Under the influence of the drugs Mary used, Nora didn't seem to recognize either of us. But she bonded with Mary — a woman-to-woman thing, I guess.

Nora and Henry were working arm-in-arm with O'Hanlon, but they were already shifting their allegiance to someone else when O'Hanlon was killed. She didn't know who the new person was. Apparently, Henry didn't share everything with her.

Nora was full of information on Frankie Dailey, too. Frankie was working for the new person, whoever he was. It was at the behest of the new person that Frankie tried to retrieve the files that his parents kept for O'Hanlon. Mary and I thought Frankie only betrayed his parents, but he sold out O'Hanlon, too. We underestimated his capacity for treachery.

That went wrong, Nora explained, when the whore hired for a threesome with Mr. and Mrs. Dailey seized the opportunity of Frankie's arrival to steal Mrs. Dailey's jewelry. The files were in the same hidden safe.

"The little slut got the files and the account codes for O'Hanlon's offshore accounts. Stupid bitch probably just raked everything out of the safe into a bag, or something," Nora said. "She was in the Dailey's bedroom. While Frankie was torturing them, she probably overheard them tell him about the hidden safe. Even the combination, he figured."

"Just dumb luck, huh?" Mary asked, egging Nora on.

"No doubt. Give her credit for being quick on her feet, though. The little vixen stole everything right out from under Frankie's nose. Then she emptied the accounts."

"So Frankie told you all this?" Mary asked.

"Yes. O'Hanlon had no clue what happened. He didn't know Frankie killed his own parents."

"But O'Hanlon must have known Frankie was there when it happened," Mary said. "How did he cover himself?"

"He told O'Hanlon he dropped in to visit his parents right after it happened. Blamed it all on the hooker; suggested that she had help. Her pimp, maybe. I don't know, exactly. But Frankie and his boys caught her."

"The hooker?" Mary asked.

"Yes. Her. But the dumb shit left her with his two guys, and whoever she was working with must have rescued her. Killed Frankie's guys. She got away."

"Really? Clean away?" Mary asked.

"For a while. But she surfaced eventually. Funny. We caught up with her by accident, but that's a long story."

"We have time," Mary said. "This is fascinating."

"Yes," Nora said. "Fascinating. Everything happened fast, with the new guy trying to take over from O'Hanlon. Kind of right in the middle of everything. Signals got crossed. It was a nightmare."

"What happened?"

"Well, Henry and I aren't gangsters, like these people. We run a super-secret, counterespionage operation. For the government."

"Awesome," Mary said. "Spies and stuff?"

"More like assassinations. We're completely off the books. This is where things get confusing. There was a man named Dimitrovsky, a Russian agent. His mission was to fund any radical organizations he could find in the U.S., just to disrupt the political process.

"He was running drugs to raise money and funneling it back to the States. Shipping in drugs, too. But the main thing was money. Anyway, we had a warrant for his execution."

"That's so amazing," Mary said. "And does this tie in with O'Hanlon?"

"Indirectly, it does. If this got out, we'd all be screwed. You follow?"

"We won't tell a soul," Mary said.

"O'Hanlon was behind the warrant. He saw Dimitrovsky as competition, and... well, O'Hanlon's connections went up much higher than me and Henry."

"Wow! So what happened?" Mary asked.

"I sent my best man to St. Vincent to kill Dimitrovsky for O'Hanlon. But boys will be boys."

"What do you mean?"

"Oh, he picked up a sleazy little girl before he left Puerto Rico and took her with him on his sailboat. Midlife crisis, I guess. But this is where it gets complicated. You still interested?"

"You bet. Keep going," Mary said.

"By then, Frankie changed sides on us — again. He was working for that new guy, the one trying to take over from O'Hanlon. But Henry and I didn't know that. You with me?"

"Yes."

"So it turns out that Dimitrovsky was working for the new guy, too. The new guy, he — "

"Do you know his name?" Mary asked.

"Who?"

"The new guy."

"Oh. No, I don't. I think Henry does, but he hasn't told me yet. Why?"

"Never mind," Mary said. "Go ahead."

"Where was I?" Nora asked.

"Frankie and Dimitrovsky both worked for the new guy."

"Oh, right. And the new guy found out we put out a kill order for Dimitrovsky. Maybe from Frankie, I don't know." Nora looked around, confused and frowning.

"It's okay," Mary said, shooting a little more of her drugs into Nora's left arm. Nora was wedged in the seat at the chart table, kept in a semi-erect position by the cushions Mary stuffed around her. Her left arm was held securely in place on the table with duct tape. A small syringe was taped to her forearm, the needle embedded in her vein and the plunger exposed.

"The new guy found out about your kill order," Mary said. "Then what?"

"He told Frankie to stop my guy from killing Dimitrovsky. But I told you, he's the best. He slipped past Frankie's people and carried out his mission. And then we got another surprise."

"What's that?"

"My guy, I told you he picked up a girl? You remember?"

"Yes. Midlife crisis," Mary said.

Nora laughed, a strange dopey laugh, and then continued. "That girl. It's the strangest thing. He asked us to get a new passport for her after they left St. Vincent. At first, we thought he was just covering his tracks with customs and immigration, changing their identities. He's good at that. But anyway, that's when we realized she wasn't just any little tramp. She was the whore that stole the files from the Daileys.

"Frankie's people let her slip through their hands twice. Once in Puerto Rico and once in the Grenadines when they were trying to stop my guy. They thought she was just a little tart he picked up."

Maybe it was that woman-to-woman thing or maybe it was the drugs, but I was amazed at how Mary established and maintained rapport with Nora. Also, I admit to being both amused and impressed by Mary's calm demeanor as Nora disparaged her repeatedly.

I reminded myself that Nora didn't realize that the solicitous young woman who hung on Nora's every word was the little slut she kept ranting about. Nor did Nora appear to be aware of my presence while Mary questioned her.

"What happened once you found the whore?" Mary asked.

"Well, Frankie planned to use O'Hanlon to catch her and get the files back. That was an easy sale; O'Hanlon was desperate for the files. When Frankie's people couldn't find my guy on his boat in Bequia — that's part of St. Vincent — they put a tracker on the boat. So it was easy to follow them to Martinique. Frankie and O'Hanlon and a bunch of O'Hanlon's people beat them there. O'Hanlon and his muscle were on Frankie's big yacht when they got there."

"When who got there?" Mary asked.

"My guy and the girl. They were on a sailboat."

"Right," Mary said. "Okay. Then what happened?"

"We don't know exactly, but we think my guy figured out somebody was after him and trapped them. Killed every damn one."

"Really?" Mary asked. "All by himself?"

"Yes. Unless maybe Frankie killed some of them. I know for a fact that my guy killed Frankie and one other one."

"For a fact?" Mary asked.

"Yes. He told me himself."

"But not the others?"

"No. I think he did, though. Probably to create a diversion, so the girl could get away."

"So she got away?"

"Yes. We lost her for a while."

"What about your guy?"

"He got away, too. I gave him another mission, so I could track him down. Met up with him in St. Martin, finally. He was in touch with the girl, but we don't know where she was.

Maybe they were both in Florida for a while, but we're not sure about anything until she showed up on his boat in Puerto Rico a few days ago."

"How did you find them there, in Puerto Rico?"

"I don't know. The new guy told us where they were. Jessie and I are on our way to meet them in Guadeloupe."

Nora clearly didn't remember her arrival in the Saintes. I wondered if that resulted from the roofies I shot her up with, or whether it was caused by whatever drug Mary was using.

"Now, who's Jessie?" Mary asked.

"Another one of my people. She's as good as Finn. Maybe better; nobody expects a woman to be a professional killer."

"And who's Finn?" Mary asked, elbowing me in the ribs.

"My guy. I'm finally going to get him in the sack after all these years. Find out what I've been missing." Nora had a vacuous grin on her face as she said that.

"What about the girl, the whore?"

"Oh, once we get the files from her, she's dead meat. Little bitch. Good riddance. She's been sleeping with Finn all this time, and all I could do was dream about him."

"Well, I guess your dream will come true. Think you'll have a happily ever after with Finn?"

"Nah. They never measure up to the fantasies; you know how that goes."

"Sounds like fun anyway, though," Mary said. "You going to let him down easy? Or break his heart?"

"Oh, honey! I'm like a praying mantis. In my line of work, I have to make sure they can't kiss and tell. I'll be his last conquest, then he's off to meet the Devil."

"Well, I'll bet he dies with a smile on his face."

"Oh, he will."

Mary grasped the syringe and injected a little more of its contents into Nora's arm, watching as she nodded off.

"She's out, now. I can bring her back if we need to. Anything else you can think of to ask her?"

"No. I think you wrung her dry. I've never seen anybody do that so well. Not your first time, for sure."

"No. I told you I had things in my past I didn't want to talk about yet. That's one. Okay?"

"Sure. What were you using?"

Mary laughed at that. "I found the drugs in the bag I took from Jessie. Well-hidden, but they were even labeled with dosages. They were probably planning to use them on you. Or me. I'm not sure what they were — the labels just illustrated the functions. One with a question mark, and the other with a thumbs-down symbol."

Mary untaped the syringe from Nora's arm and injected the contents of a second syringe into her vein.

"She's done. By the time we get her on deck, she'll be gone, I imagine. I gave her way more of the thumbs-down shot than the label called for. Bitch. She pissed me off. Let's clean up the boat. I'm starving."

39

I FIGURED AARON COULD TELL US ALL WE NEEDED TO KNOW
about Nora's boss, now that we knew his name and title.
Henry Jacobs was on my shit list now. I wasn't sure how
Mary felt about him yet.

We were both hungry; we missed lunch, and then we
spent a couple of hours debriefing Nora. I was looking
forward to comparing notes with Mary while we ate.

With Nora out of the way, Mary volunteered to cook. I
could tell from the aroma wafting up into the cockpit that
dinner was about ready. Sure enough, in a few minutes she
appeared in the companionway with two steaming bowls of
saltfish curry.

"Hungry?" she asked, handing me a bowl.

"Famished. Thanks."

"My pleasure. You know I was just teasing you, right?
Back there at the ferry dock when I got on your case about
groping Nora?"

I gave her what I meant to be a lascivious grin. "Can't fool
me. Your jealousy was showing."

"Wiseass. I'll show you a thing or two. But not right now. Let's eat."

"Okay," I said. "Right before you came ashore I saw the ferry captain and two other men scurry below with a first aid kit. I'm guessing they were going to clean up after your hit."

"Probably. There wasn't much to clean up, though. Jessie went into the women's head just before we docked. I followed her in. Nobody else was there, and I stuck her when she was coming out of the stall. Pushed her back in, arranged the body — artistically, I might add — locked the stall, and crawled under the door. It was an ugly hit, but quick. I've never used potassium chloride before this."

"Yeah, it gets the job done. But you're right. It's not fun to see somebody die that way. You can tell it's not painless."

"Guess that's why they add the anesthetic and muscle relaxant when they execute people by lethal injection," Mary said.

"Right. The problem is, those things will show up in a post-mortem."

"But not the potassium chloride, you said."

"Well, it does show up. But it's expected. An elevated potassium level is common in deaths from cardiac arrest. It rises anytime muscles get overworked. That includes the heart muscles."

"I'll remember that for later."

"Later?"

"To make sure I don't wear you out too much."

I chuckled, and we ate in silence for a few minutes.

"What do you think we should do about this Henry Jacobs?" Mary asked, when she finished her bowl of curry.

"Kill him."

"Well, duh! I figured that. How are we going to get to him?"

"I figured we could talk that over with Aaron once we got settled at Isla de Aves."

She nodded. "So are you going to call him? Jacobs? Let him know you accomplished your mission?"

"I've been thinking about that. I haven't decided yet. What do you think?"

"I don't know. That's what you'd do if you were innocent."

I burst out laughing at that.

Mary grinned. "Well, damn it, you know what I mean. Innocent's not the right word."

"No, it sure isn't. But yes, I know what you mean. If I believed everything he told me the other day, I would call in to let him know I took care of his rogue agent for him. And fill him in on what I learned from her, I guess. But he sent her down here to kill me. We both know that."

"He had to at least consider the possibility that you'd turn the tables on her, Finn. He knows your track record."

"Yes, I agree. That's why I might call him; to see what his next move will be. And I want to know more about the woman he sent with Nora before I talk to him. I wasn't supposed to kill her, remember? In his version of the story, she was going to turn Nora over to me and leave. So whatever I decide about Henry Jacobs, I won't call him until after I give Aaron a chance to check up on him and — what was her name, anyway? Besides just Jessie, I mean."

"I don't know. But we've got all their luggage. Hang on." Mary took our empty bowls below and returned with a small gym bag, plus Nora's shoulder bag.

"I didn't see you with the gym bag when you got off the ferry," I said.

"I stuffed it in my backpack after I killed her. Let's see what she was carrying."

"I thought you searched it. You said that's where you got the drugs you used on Nora."

"I went through it quickly once we got back to the boat with Nora. I wanted to make sure there wasn't a tracker or something hidden in it, in case she and Nora had backup."

"That's when you found the drugs?"

"Yes. I still can't believe they only sent those two to kill you. Nora kept saying you were their best."

"Two against one's decent odds," I said. "Even if both of them were female."

"Trying to pick a fight?" Mary asked.

"Just teasing you. You teased me about groping her, but she started that. I'm sure it was planned. She was going to invite me into her room at whatever resort she booked herself into. While she was having her way with me, her pal Jessie would have put me away."

"That was obvious. But Nora just got through telling us you were the best they had. You really think she was that sure of herself with you? You two have a history you haven't told me about?"

"No. No history. But she did lay it on heavy in St. Martin. Then she backed off, teasing me, like."

"You didn't tell me that."

"I thought she was just flirtatious. But now it looks to be part of a longer-term plan to get me to drop my guard."

"More like to drop your pants," Mary said, smirking.

"Maybe so. But like I said, I want to check out this Jessie woman. If she's not really one of their top killers, then there's probably somebody looking for us in the Saintes about now. It's been long enough so Nora or Jessie one would have checked in with somebody."

Mary nodded and unzipped Jessie's gym bag, dumping the contents on the cockpit seat. There were a few clothes: a bikini; fresh shorts and T-shirt; undergarments; a small, zippered bag of toiletries. Mary picked up a paper airline folder holding a passport and return tickets. Opening the passport, she held it so we could both see it.

"Jessica Ellen Kirkman," she said. "That's a good likeness, for a passport picture."

"I see what you mean about her being nondescript," I said.

"Yes. She wasn't remarkable. You could fix her up, and she'd look good, but not good enough to attract attention."

"No weapon," I said, pawing through the contents of her bag.

"She just got off an airplane, Finn."

"But there was plenty of opportunity for her to arm herself between the airport and the ferry terminal."

"What's your point?" Mary asked.

"Still worrying about whether there was a third person. Maybe somebody already on the ground in the Saintes. All they would have needed was a local contact to give them a weapon. It's odd that she had the drugs and nothing else. Was she wearing any jewelry?"

"A plain-looking, heavy gold-chain necklace. Probably worth a good bit. And a heavy ring on her right hand."

"Ah," I said. "The chain would make a garrote. Probably gold-plated high-tensile steel, and I would bet the ring was loaded with something. It probably had a retracted needle. You've never seen one of those?"

Mary shook her head. "No. Not my style. I'm not into

gimmicks. Anyhow, I always thought that was just spy movie stuff."

"Yeah," I said. "But there really are such things. They date back to the Middle Ages, at least. I wouldn't be surprised if she and Nora had some help waiting in the wings, though. Aaron can probably find out."

"Does it matter at this point?"

"It could. You can't be too careful dealing with people like these. They have almost unlimited resources."

Mary scooped the things back into Jessie's bag. Unzipping Nora's shoulder bag, she dumped out its contents. Nora wasn't carrying anything interesting, other than her passport. This one was in the name of Nora Anne Lewis.

"I wonder what her real name was," Mary said.

I shrugged. "Probably nobody but Henry Jacobs knows. I don't think I'll ask him, though."

"It's early yet," Mary said. "Think you can reach Aaron tonight?"

"It's worth a try."

I took Nora and Jessie's passports below and came back up with my laptop and the hotspot.

"While I fire this stuff up, why don't you get a few heavy sinkers out of the fishing tackle box and weight those bags? No need in hanging onto them."

40

BEFORE I CALLED AARON, I CHECKED OUR BLIND EMAIL DROP. That was just as well, because I found a new phone number for Aaron. There was more to his message, but I figured it was no longer as critical as he thought it was. It was from almost 24 hours earlier. A lot happened since then.

Call me at the number in the subject line ASAP. You're in trouble again.

"In trouble again," Mary said, poking me in the ribs as she read over my shoulder. "He knows you, doesn't he?"

"He does."

I shut down the laptop and got my Wi-Fi-only iPhone connected to the hot spot. Keying in his new number, I soon heard his gruff answer.

"Yeah?"

"Sorry for the delayed response. Things have been crazy. You say I'm in trouble again?"

"Yeah. Our friend Nora's headed your way with a warrant for your execution. You somewhere around Guadeloupe? Word is, she's bringing help. But I don't know who."

"Jessica Ellen Kirkman," I said.

"Who's that?"

"The help Nora brought. I want you to see what you can find out about her. I'll leave a photo of her passport in the email drop for you. And yes, I was in Guadeloupe."

"Did they catch you?"

"Yes, they did."

"Sounds like it didn't go the way Nora planned, then." Aaron chuckled.

"I don't know. Maybe they were tired of living. Anyhow, they won't bother us again. I would like the background on Jessica, though. Jessie, Nora called her. Said she was one of the best. Maybe even better than me."

"I guess Nora was wrong about that," Aaron said.

"I don't know. I didn't get to meet Jessie before she died."

"What happened? You still hiding behind your lady friend's skirts?"

"When I can, you bet."

"Did she save your ass from Nora, too?"

"Nora was so excited to see me she swooned in my arms. But Mary *did* help me make her comfortable. Oh, and on a serious note, Nora gave us the name and title of her boss. Thought we might want to let him know what happened to her."

"You gonna make me beg?"

"Just ask nicely."

"Please?" Aaron asked, dragging it out.

I gave him the details, but I wasn't ready for his response. "Holy shit, Finn!"

"Don't tell me you know the guy," I said.

"Hardly. But you don't need to worry about him. He's history. Dead, dead and gone."

"Really? I talked to him the day before yesterday."

"You would have been one of the last, then. He was one of those people who didn't exist as far as DOD was concerned. There won't be any news releases about this, but it's pretty friggin' scary."

"What happened to him?"

"He was found in his home office in the D.C. suburbs by his housekeeper."

"Suicide?" I asked.

"Unlikely. I don't see how it could be. Never heard of a zamochit suicide."

"Whoa. So much for my plans to visit him. Guess he pissed off his Russian overlord."

"Yeah. Look, I was about to leave you another message, but since you're on the line, I'll just tell you. We cracked the code for that list your lady stole."

"Great. What's it look like?"

"Well, we're working out what to do with it. It will take a while to sort through it all. But I need to talk with you about a related matter."

"What's that?"

"Your career plans. Looks like you've lost your cushy government job. What's next for you?"

"Yeah, I figure I'm out of work. I haven't thought much about it yet. Why did you want to talk?"

"You interested in an opportunity to make a difference? Improve things for the good ol' US of A?"

"Maybe. What happens if I say yes?"

"I need you to trust me enough to say yes. It's the right thing for you, and I'm already in. Okay?"

"Okay."

"That's a yes?"

"Yes."

"Good. I was counting on that. Your lady friend there?"

"Her name's Mary. Most of the time, anyway."

"Okay. Mary. Is she there?"

"Yes."

"Can you put her on with us?"

"You sure about that, Aaron?"

"Absolutely. I trust her, even though I've never met her. You'll know why in a few seconds."

"Okay, then. Mary, say hello to Aaron."

"Hello, Aaron."

"Hi. Pleased to meet you. I need for you both to hold on for a second while I add someone to our call."

"Go for it," I said.

A second later, there was a click, and a man's voice said, "Medusa? Phorcys here."

Mary and I traded stunned glances. She swallowed hard and cleared her throat.

"Phorcys, Medusa."

"Good. And is Abigail's father on the line?"

"I'm here," I said.

"Excellent," Phorcys said. "You don't know me, but I've followed your career since your early days."

"You have?" I asked, wondering who he could be.

"I have. The man who replaced me when I retired told me you and Aaron were the best junior officers who ever served under him. And he was outstanding himself. He was the youngest general officer on active duty when he assumed command of my old unit."

"That would have to be Bob Lawson," I said.

"Correct. He picked you and Aaron out to recruit before he even assumed command."

"And that would make you — "

"Yes, it would. You know who I am. Bob wanted to welcome you aboard himself, but he's busy elsewhere right now. We're both pleased to have you with us."

"Thank you, sir. It's an honor."

"Yes. I'm honored to be in such company myself. Hate to cut this short, but I'm running late, so here's your first assignment. Ready?"

"Yes, sir."

"You can drop the sir. We're all in this together. I want you and Medusa to go somewhere private and take it easy for a few days. While you're resting, share everything you know about us with each other. Medusa's got a lot of recent background, but she will be surprised by some of what you tell her, Finn. You still answer to Finn?"

"I do."

"Good. Everybody calls me Mike now. If you have questions that one or the other of you can't answer, talk to Aaron. Just like always, he knows everything about everything worth knowing. And Medusa?"

"Yes?"

"You know how to reach me. Nothing's changed about our relationship. It's just that now you have two more people you can trust with our business. Okay?"

"Yes. Thank you."

"You're welcome. And I'm still indebted to you. Good evening, y'all. Carry on."

And with that, he was gone.

"How long, Aaron?" I asked.

"How long have I been working with Phorcys?"

"Yes. That's my question."

"I've been trading information with them since I left

Bob's command, but I didn't know they were Phorcys — just some of my regular contacts. They only brought me into the fold since the business with Nora blew up. Looking back on it, though, it was a gradual transition.

"I wasn't holding out on you earlier, Finn. My answers were honest at the time. This happened in the last few days, the big switch. Mostly, they didn't have to tell me much. Just confirmed what I already picked up along the way. It's probably going to be the same with you — both of you. Welcome to Phorcys."

"Thanks. I'm sure we'll have questions, once we compare notes."

"No doubt. I'll answer what I can, but I have to tell you up front that Phorcys is organized in cells. We three only know one another and Mike and Bob, for sure. They know a few others. But beyond that, there isn't much I can tell you. Most of us are retired military. But not all, unless I missed something about you, Mary."

"No. I was never in the military, but I have a question for you."

"Ask away," Aaron said.

"What about the files?" Mary asked. "What will happen with them? The people, I mean?"

"They're all politicians or career bureaucrats. We'll investigate and categorize them. That's started already. Some will be turned over to the authorities, assuming the authorities pass muster. Some will be outed in the press or social media and forced to withdraw from whatever they're screwing up. But the worst ones will be prioritized for elimination."

"That's where we come in, I guess," Mary said. "The vigilante squad."

"Yes, but only in the best sense of the word 'vigilante.' I

know Finn's okay with that, and I'm guessing that if you weren't, you wouldn't already be called Medusa."

"I'm okay with it."

"If you have questions, call me. Meanwhile, fair winds, and enjoy your holiday. Keep checking that email drop. I expect things will break on the files in about a week."

With that, we disconnected the call.

"I guess I won't be talking with Henry Jacobs," I said, looking at Mary.

"No. I guess you won't."

"So, do I get to call you Medusa now?"

"Call me whatever you want. But I like it when you call me Mary."

"Then I'll call you Mary."

"Are we going to stand watches?" Mary asked.

"Sure. If you want to crash, go for it. I'm too wound up to sleep."

She smiled and shook her head. "Me, too. How about if I make us a pot of coffee? Sounds like we have a lot to talk about."

"Coffee would be great," I said.

41

A FEW MINUTES LATER, MARY WAS SNUGGLED UNDER MY ARM. We sipped our coffee while I steered into the sunset with my foot on the tiller.

"You must have a thousand questions for me, Finn."

"I don't know about a thousand. But I do have a few."

"Is it okay if I ask you one, first?"

"Yes. Go ahead."

"Who is he? The man I've been dealing with?"

"Lieutenant General Michael Killington. Retired from the Army right before I began reporting to Bob Lawson. He's a legend. He was nicknamed Killer Mike. There are a lot of stories about how he got the nickname, but not much doubt about whether he deserved it. He led covert missions in the field — I mean with a bloody knife in his hand — right up until he retired. He would have to be in his 70s now. But I wouldn't want to tangle with him."

"I knew Phorcys was the organization's name, not his. But that's all I ever called him. Mike, huh? I'll be awhile getting used to that."

"You and I both will," I said. "He said your relationship with him was unchanged by this. What is your relationship?"

"Well, it started out like I told you, but for about the last year, I've been an exclusive contractor to Phorcys. They've been paying me to pass up other jobs."

"I see. So you weren't part of Phorcys?"

"No. I didn't know anything about them, except that I always dealt with the same person. I would get a message to call a certain number and ask for Phorcys. When I identified myself as Medusa, the man we're calling Mike would answer. Same deal if I needed anything from them — like when I asked for help with Abby. Why are you frowning, Finn?"

"Because it's strange that an organization made up of people like Mike Killington would hire an outsider, a contract killer."

"I think I know the answer to that. And I'm not sure I like it."

"Really?" I raised my eyebrows. "Let's hear it."

"First, you served under this Bob Lawson, right?"

"Yes. Why?"

"Would he be in his mid-fifties, now?"

"He could be. I don't know exactly how old he was back then, but he was young, like Mike said. The youngest general officer in the Army."

"And do you know his full name?"

"Robert James Lawson."

"It has to be him," Mary said. "I can't believe it, but there's no way it can't be him. No way it's a coincidence."

"Okay, come clean. Him who?"

"Finn, I'm... he's got to be my uncle. My mother's older brother. I told you she was a druggie, right?"

"Yes."

"She was far worse than just a casual user, but let's skip that. They were estranged, she and my uncle. But he tried to straighten her out every so often. Long sad story. When she finally overdosed, I was 12. I went into foster care. That's a whole horror story, but the short version is I ran away. I was on my own before I was 13."

"Bob didn't help you?"

"No. Not then. I didn't even know him. Just that my mother had a brother who tried to help her. And she didn't want his help. I only have a few vague memories of him coming around when I was little.

"He apparently had people, private detectives, looking for me, after she died. But they didn't find me until I was in college. And I was already hooked up with the broker by then."

"So what happened?"

"I was an angry young bitch, then. I was super pissed-off that he didn't help me before. He told me he was in the Middle East when my mother died and didn't find out until after I bailed out of the foster care system."

"What did you say to that?"

"I told him to go fuck himself. I didn't need his help, and I didn't want him in my life."

"You think he engineered this deal with Phorcys?" I asked.

"He must have."

"He was famous for never taking no for an answer," I said. "This is the sort of thing he would do."

"I'm at a loss, Finn."

"Why? Still angry after all this time?"

"No, I got over that, even regretted treating him that way, after I cooled off. But now I feel like I've been manipulated."

"Everybody gets manipulated, one way or another. Sounds like he was trying to take care of you."

"Yes. But it will take me some time to get my head around this. Do you know him well?"

"I did, but that was a long time ago. You would have been maybe three or four, then. He was my commanding officer for around 18 months. When I came back from the dead, he had moved on. I always suspected he had a hand in my getting moved to the group that Nora ended up running."

"He wasn't the one who recruited you to go there, then?"

"No. It was another man I served with. He was probably Mike's age; he was the unit's executive officer. Then he retired and moved to the DOD to start the group. I was one of his first recruits."

"I don't know what to think, Finn."

"I can understand that. But you're in a good place to take your time and figure things out. I'll give you all the space you need."

"You're so good to me. I don't need space. Not from you. I need you to help me figure this out. What do you think about it all?"

"Mike sent you to look after me. With what I know now, I think they were betting we'd team up. I don't think any of this is an accident."

"Don't you feel used, Finn? Manipulated?"

"Yes. But I'm accustomed to it. I've been used and manipulated for better than 20 years. But I'm okay with that; I consented to it. I let myself be used to do things that are important. Remember, some folks just need killin'. That's what we do, you and I."

"We do make a good team," she said.

"Yes. And I'm excited about the idea that we're working

for the same people. I like it. You seemed to be comfortable with Phorcys."

"That's so. I was. I am."

"Well, it's like Mike said. That part hasn't changed for you. Not really. And we can work together without trying to hide stuff from one another. It's all good, the way I see it."

"You trust them?"

"Yes. I surely do."

She nodded. "How is this business with my uncle going to come out?"

"That's up to the two of you. How do you want it to come out?"

"I don't know. I want it to come out so you and I are together."

"We already are."

"I mean long-term," she said.

"I'd like that; that's what I want, too. We'll make it happen."

"Thanks, Finn. I think I can sleep, now," she said. "You okay for a while?"

"Yes. See you in a few hours."

She gave me a kiss and went below.

EPILOGUE

MARY AND I SPENT FOUR DAYS AT ISLA DE AVES. SHE GOT USED to the idea that she didn't have to fight all her battles alone.

And we discovered that being alone together on a desert island wasn't quite paradise. We were running low on fresh water, starting to think about where to go from there. Then we got a message from Aaron. We had our first assignment.

We set off from Isla de Aves on a broad reach, and 30 hours later, we put *Island Girl* in a marina in Fajardo. Mary took a nonstop flight from San Juan to Miami the next morning.

I stayed behind to get the boat squared away. We expected to be in the States for several weeks. There was a lot of work to be done. Mary was taking care of the logistics and preliminary reconnaissance for our first official job together. After another day of working on *Island Girl*, I planned to fly to Miami to join her.

Mary was excited. Me, I was a happy man. A job is just a job, but the people you work with make all the difference. I was going to miss living on the boat for a while, but I would have a *real* island girl to keep me company.

MAILING LIST

Thank you for reading *Vigilantes and Lovers*.

Sign up for my mailing list at http://eepurl.com/bKujyv for notice of new releases and special sales or giveaways. I'll email a link to you for a free download of my short story, The Lost Tourist Franchise, when you sign up. I promise not to use the list for anything else; I dislike spam as much as you do.

A NOTE TO THE READER

Thank you again for reading *Vigilantes and Lovers*, the third book in the **J.R. Finn Sailing Mystery Series.** I hope you enjoyed it. If so, please leave a brief review on Amazon.

Reviews are of great benefit to independent authors like me; they help me more than you can imagine. They are a primary means to help new readers find my work. A few words from you can help others find the pleasure that I hope you found in this book, as well as keeping my spirits up as I work on the next one.

The **J.R Finn Sailing Mystery Series** is also available in audiobook format.

————

I also write two other sailing-thriller series set in the Caribbean. If you enjoyed the adventures of Finn and Mary, you'll enjoy the **Bluewater Thrillers** and the **Connie Barrera Thrillers.**

The **Bluewater Thrillers** feature two young women, Dani Berger and Liz Chirac. Dani and Liz sail a luxury charter yacht named *Vengeance*. They often find trouble, but they can take care of themselves.

The **Connie Barrera Thrillers** are a spin-off from the **Bluewater Thrillers**. Before Connie went to sea, she was a first-rate con artist. Dani and Liz met Connie in *Bluewater Ice*, and they taught her to sail. She liked it so much she bought a charter yacht of her own.

Dani and Liz also introduced her to Paul Russo, a retired Miami homicide detective. Paul signed on as her first mate and chef, but he ended up as her husband. Connie and Paul run a charter sailing yacht named *Diamantista*. Like Dani and Liz, they're often beset by problems unrelated to sailing.

The **Bluewater Thrillers** and the **Connie Barrera Thrillers** share many of the same characters. Phillip Davis and his wife Sandrine, Sharktooth, and Marie LaCroix often appear in both series, as do Connie, Paul, Dani, and Liz. Here's a link to the web page that lists those novels in order of publication: http://www.clrdougherty.com/p/bluewater-thrillers-and-connie-barrera.html

———

A list of all my books is on the last page; just click on a title or go to my website for more information. If you'd like to know when my next book is released, visit my author's page on Amazon at www.amazon.com/author/clrdougherty and click the "Follow" link or sign up for my mailing list at http://eepurl.com/bKujyv for information on sales and special promotions.

I welcome email correspondence about books, boats and sailing. My address is <u>clrd@clrdougherty.com</u>. I enjoy hearing from people who read my books; I always answer email from readers. Thanks again for your support.

ABOUT THE AUTHOR

Welcome Aboard!

Charles Dougherty is a lifelong sailor; he's lived what he writes. He and his wife have spent over 30 years sailing together.

For 15 years, they lived aboard their boat full-time, cruising the East Coast and the Caribbean islands. They spent most of that time exploring the Eastern Caribbean.

Dougherty is well acquainted with the islands and their people. The characters and locations in his novels reflect his experience.

A storyteller before all else, Dougherty lets his characters speak for themselves. Pick up one of his thrillers and listen to the sound of adventure as you smell the salt air. Enjoy the views of distant horizons and meet some people you won't forget.

Dougherty's sailing fiction books include the **Bluewater Thrillers**, the **Connie Barrera Thrillers**, and the **J.R. Finn Sailing Mysteries**.

Dougherty's first novel was *Deception in Savannah*. While it's not about sailing, one of the main characters is Connie Barrera. He had so much fun with Connie that he built a sailing series around her.

Before writing Connie's series, he wrote the first three

Bluewater Thrillers, about two young women running a charter yacht in the islands. In the fourth book, Connie shows up as their charter guest.

She stayed for the fifth Bluewater book. Then Connie demanded her own series.

The J.R. Finn books are his newest sailing series. The first Finn book, though it begins in Puerto Rico, starts with a real-life encounter that Dougherty had in St. Lucia. For more information about that, visit his website.

Dougherty's other fiction works are the *Redemption of Becky Jones*, a psycho-thriller, and *The Lost Tourist Franchise*, a short story about another of the characters from Deception in Savannah.

Dougherty has also written two non-fiction books. *Life's a Ditch* is the story of how he and his wife moved aboard their sailboat, Play Actor, and their adventures along the east coast of the U.S. *Dungda de Islan'* relates their experiences while cruising the Caribbean.

Charles Dougherty welcomes email correspondence with readers.

www.clrdougherty.com
clrd@clrdougherty.com

Books for Sailors and Dreamers

Life's a Ditch

Dungda de Islan'

Audiobooks

Assassins and Liars

Avengers and Rogues

Vigilantes and Lovers

Sailors and Sirens

Villains and Vixens

Killers and Keepers

Devils and Divas

Sharks and Prey

For more information please visit www.clrdougherty.com

Or visit www.amazon.com/author/clrdougherty

Made in the USA
Las Vegas, NV
01 March 2022